*To Maurice Cottingham,
with best wishes,*

Charles E. Eaton

WRITE

ME

FROM

RIO

WRITE ME FROM RIO...

AND YOU'LL KEEP YOUR PLEDGE;

I KNOW YOUR WORD!

Hart Crane, The Bridge

CHARLES EDWARD EATON

WRITE ME FROM RIO

1959
JOHN F. BLAIR, Publisher
Winston-Salem

ACKNOWLEDGMENTS

Acknowledgments are due to the following
magazines for permission to reprint the stories:
Epoch, The Southwest Review, Prairie Schooner
The Georgia Review, Shenandoah, Folio
The University of Kansas City Review
Damernas Varld (Sweden), *The Northern Review* (Canada)
Meanjin (Australia), *Arbiter,* (England), *Senhor* (Brazil)

"The Motion of Forgetfulness is Slow" was also reprinted in
Martha Foley's *The Best American Short Stories of 1952*
(Houghton-Mifflin Co.)

TO ISABEL

CONTENTS

THE RIVER OF WINGS

YOU MIGHT HAVE SAID I WAS A HUNTER AMONG MY own people, or, if you were kind, a collector of national specimens, a connoisseur of the American abroad. I suppose—looking back on it now—I did spend most of my time in Rio doing just that. I never took much of a look at the Brazilians themselves. They were so much folk-foliage in a land too lush, the animate landscape—nature, at best, was always cloying to me in the end. As a matter of fact I was soon tired of the blatant heroics of the Brazilian earth; I had thought it would help me forget myself, but, on the contrary, I found that at first it made me want to talk back like a pigmy growing hoarse among giants. Soon this passed, for I discovered that the land and the people, really one continuum, were of such somnolent indifference that anything I said about them was lost in their languid dream.

But, ah, there were the Americans, my compatriots. If it had not been for them, the War in Brazil would have indeed been overlong, and I should have been frozen in the tropics in a way that a land of ice and snow never makes one feel. But, oh, the Americans, thank God for them! The War brought a great influx, "the American invasion," so spoken of in some quarters, as though the golden swarm might turn out to be a pestilence. And all of them passed through Rio, caught for a few days, a week, or a month or so, in its glimmering net of enchantment before stuffing themselves once more into the gorged, overcrowded planes and taking wing for São Paulo, some dim little town in the provinces, or perhaps back home. In any event, opportunity for me was rife. I met them everywhere: in the streets, the shops, the clubs, on the beach, in the parks, at Embassy receptions, at the U.S.O. . . . everywhere . . . and discovered, as always, that you could strike up with an American anywhere and have him give you his story in five minutes, and this was what I was after—life history! I had found a hobby. The fellow who at home would undoubtedly have been a boor and a nuisance seemed here only a cruder but no less interesting example in the collection. I grew positively acquisitive as time went on and found myself expending no small effort and sometimes undergoing inconvenience to be sure I didn't miss out, that I was on hand when I got wind of the fact that some rare one had flown into town. The days went rapidly then as my inventory increased. It was as though I was hoarding this stock of personalities to be stirred together in the alembic of an Idea—What is an American?—the distillation to be poured out at last in a glass, its bouquet, body, and potency noted, then bottled up forever.

In any case, I classified my fellows endlessly, meticulously—I might say fastidiously, a word more than any other I should like to have applied to myself. I compartmentalized them into Exteriors, how a man looked and what he pretended to be, and Interiors, what a man really was, the contradiction of his behavior and belief, the fact, perhaps, that he was in Brazil for one reason when he said he was there for another. I was not particularly interested in "bridges" since they seemed to complicate the division, and I was looking for crystallizations. You might say that composition bored me with its impenetrable unity whereas components could easily be assorted and put away.

It was in the interest of my science one June afternoon that I went to the Saturday matinée of the Brazilian Ballet at the Teatro Municipal. I detest matinées, crowded as they usually are with squirming, noisy children, but I had read in the *Correio da Manhã* that the ballet was using several American imports as

4

sustaining members of the corps this year and that one of them, a Miss Margot Anthony, was a dancer of promise. This was a chance to meet an artist in Brazil—I had been gathering too many of late in the same monotonous category: business enterprise. Besides, I was something of a balletomane, having been drawn to it by my earlier appreciation of the art of Dégas; an incomparable painter to me, fastidious in the highest sense of the word, a perfect *maître d'illusion*—one could see that meant everything to him: the elegance and fineness of his calculation; and I loathed romantic criticism which made him like itself: soft and fuzzy as if he swooned into his feelings for his subject, as if he cared in that way.

I was glad to find that it was an off day for children—there would be peace after all. I was tired, in one of my black moods, and the dark, gloomy vault of the old opera house was a magnification of my mind which was glad to have its interior lit and warmed by the spectacle on the stage filtering radiance through the eyes like sunrays into a cave.

Without looking at my program, I could have spotted Margot Anthony. Her vitality was remarkable amid the apparent lassitude and routine movement of the others. At every climax of motion, she rose higher than the rest, hovering for an instant above them in a cloud of yellow, silver, and white, and landing softer as if the floor were a bumper of rubber. Her levitation was superb—always the mark of a natural dancer—she seemed to have wings everywhere, in the flying gold of her hair, her shoulders, in the brisk twinkling of her *entrechat,* the flung dervish of her *tour en l'air.* She was really too beautiful for words! I could almost have allowed myself the sentimental "Ah" of the audience's devotion, but lost myself in the study of her perfect technique. This was the nth power of acrobatics. It was the same faultless thrill I had derived from the aerialist at the circus in his white tights, swinging, soaring, turning, descending, almost but never falling, a sky-dance of incredible purity, arabesques of motion for the eye of the formalist.

5

When the performance had wound itself back into its source behind the curtains, mainly for me on the shining thread of this young American's exquisite motion, so that she seemed to weave among the other dancers as through a labyrinth of heavy flesh, I knew what I should do. Though the role of stage-door Johnny made me cringe, I must add Margot Anthony to my American collection, for she promised to be *outré*, out of the ordinary, a little touch of lovely extravagance to give a fillip to the recent desuetude of my studies.

I had no trouble seeing her—apparently she didn't have many callers. When my name was announced to her, she opened the door immediately. "So you're an American too. Do come in." She shook my hand effusively and asked eagerly, "You liked the performance?"

"I most certainly did, Miss Anthony," I said with just the proper amount of restraint, I hoped. "You were the life of the whole thing."

"That's wonderful to hear," she said, trying to check her effervescence. "I had hoped someone from back home would be in the audience. They are so kind down here. They say such marvelous things in the newspapers. But you never know. Have you noticed that a compliment in a foreign language always sounds a little unreal? It puts a lot of fuzz around it somehow."

She smiled, and I had the clearest impression of her mobility even when she was standing still. It was *stored* in her, this kinetic spool of lucid gesture and floating strength. I noticed that there was a light perspiration on her face, arms, and hands, which, far from being unattractive, seemed to give her an extra sheen and glow like the oil of active beauty, the luxuriance of motion.

The settings of people were always important to me, and I glanced searchingly around the dressing room and found it a dreary, grimy little socket for the issuance of all this radiance. You could see she didn't care. There was not a picture on the wall, not an adornment of any sort. She had taken it as it was, her only contribution the little pots of cosmetics in spattered

6

disarray and her costumes hung in the corner like bright, magical sacks of the arrested dance. As she stood in her fragile-metallic light, there was not a trace of conflict in her face to reveal a fear of the miasmic interpenetration of one world and another. This was the stage still, I could sense that, and she was out there what she was here, her attitude imposing without trying its natural validity. She didn't need a background!

I waited outside until she had finished dressing, and received another shock when she appeared in street clothes. It was as if all that golden effulgence had been folded tightly into a sheath of gray, the flowing arms, the buoyant, mercurial legs bound into the taut measure of a worn, tailored suit, with only her blonde hair and her face spilling out like an overflow of what I remembered. I was a little annoyed. She didn't need to look so dowdy; she owed something to the rest of us who stood looking down into the gap, who saw only too plainly the hideous yawn at the center of things.

But I was determined not to give up; I would "have" her at any cost, and I invited her for tea the following afternoon since it was Sunday and I presumed that she would have some time to herself. She accepted without hesitation, seeming to think it was the most natural thing in the world to do, and I left her in front of the theatre waiting for her bus, thin as a pencil with a gold knob at the tip, the sort that fate, when its hand is impelled by a nisus of crudity, could break as a hasty means of unwrapping and scattering the lode of brightness.

I walked home alone in the wistful tropic winter afternoon on the promenade along the sea, feeling the currents of coolness breathe in from the water and down the mountains. It was just before twilight, late enough for brooding, and I gave myself over to my natural inclination. This so-called "winter weather" always affected me thus. The corridors of the city were like a draughty conservatory left open to some far-wandering northern breeze. It was not enough to kill; it would never bring snow, a freezing decision of death in nature and the chance to start all over again. No, it was a suspension in the sun of the mildest

7

sort, and the blent coolness and attenuated warmth was a sus-
piration of the earth under an eternal burden of green and
flowers, knowing that this was a pause, not a stop, tired of its
destiny as an unbroken nexus of growth but certain that it
could have no other. This is like autumn in the States, I
thought, without the longing and the expectation of death and
birth, without the immortal possibility of being born entirely
new again come spring.

It was beautiful, though, like being caught in a globe of
mellow sunlight tinctured with dankness, a fruit, however, that
would never fall, that would simply melt from the mind of the
world as the sun grew warm once more around it. As I walked
along, I let myself swing in the melancholy, false-October sum-
mary suffusion. I thought of Margot. I thought of how little she
seemed to succumb to the world around her. But this was ridiculous, of course, an evening nostalgia. She was probably as mal-
leable as a sheet of foil once one knew her, with a perfectly
tawdry little soul in a glorious body. I would find out tomorrow
—she would turn out to be nothing but a chorus girl with airs—
"artistic integrity," she would call it. But why the "airs," why
should they be at all? That would be interesting. That, at least,
would be a project for tomorrow.

Already I felt weakly fond of her, and I could not excuse
myself, for I was proud of my usual detachment from my subjects. Perhaps it was the fact that she was a dancer. Yes, I had a
failing in that direction. Though I told myself it was an inferior
art—it was a bodily and ephemeral thing and died with the
individual, even its technique embedded and so lost in the
corporeal—I had found myself time and again in the States on
gray winter days drawn to the ballet theatres as though those
soaring and rubescent girls exuded a fountain of warmth which
one had some indefinable necessity for hovering about. But I
scoffed at it all; it was nothing but the sedentary self in search
of physical bounce. That was what it was again with Margot.
She was a charming bauble to titillate the lagging rhythm of
my life. It was sheer acrobatics I needed! That was what she was

8

even in repose, animal spark and spunk, a transfusion of life for languid veins.

When I reached my apartment, I was truly tired with the "given-over-to-whatever-gods-may-be" exhaustion I had experienced only in Brazil. The damn country had simply flattened me at last, I decided. It had bludgeoned me with its sensory hammer day after day, and what had I gotten for my intellectual resistance? Nothing but this fatigue over all—yes, it had gotten me in the end. But, tonight, in contrast to all of this bodily defeat, there was Margot. I put her away in the fastness of a velvet corner of consciousness like a sparkling, jeweled trinket that might leap up and take flight, so alive it was. Yes, she was like a dazzling ornament which that lavish woman, the imagination, might wear on her lapel as she walked through the world, flaunting her magic and her courage.

Sunday was another classic winter afternoon, flawlessly clear, lightly swept with a northern emanation, laden with imponderables, and by four o'clock, when we met, the sense of shadow from the great mountains around the city was tall in the mind, increasing the feeling of being very far away at the ends of the earth, at the mercy of nature, which this time of the year in Brazil inspires. We had agreed to meet at the teashop on the Praia Flamengo, A Sala Dourada, an old haunt of mine to which I often brought my American acquaintances, particularly women. After the style of cafés in Paris, it had tables outside along the walk under the almond trees, but I usually preferred to sit inside where one could get the vista of the sea through the open window and still feel sufficiently inclosed to get a cozy feeling which, I discovered, was one of the things one missed in the tropics. The interior glimmered with tones of brown and gold and was just right for a coolish afternoon, just intimate enough for tea with a charming young lady. Everyone at the establishment knew me—as a matter of fact, you might have said it was a kind of lair of mine, and I liked the noiseless, gracious attendants who wove their fine threads of service in a network around my well-being. This conspiratorial ease abetted me in

9

ensnaring whoever was with me in a cage of his own relaxation, one with wide spaces between the rods, but nevertheless a containment where I had him swinging on the bar of my subtle questioning.

Margot wore the same rumpled gray suit, and I could see that she hadn't made any effort to glamorize herself for our meeting. But it didn't matter, though it did upset my balance of calculation and drew me rather into the cage as well as she. I noticed her gray eyes this time, cool and white in their depths so that they took you in with their unmoted ingenuousness. She was more fragile and slender than I had remembered, since her strength on the stage was superb. But it was once again her extraordinary bodily animation even at rest which lured the hand to hold her into place—something supraterrestrial, not bird-like with snake-glint in the eyes, some muted, atavistic note of rapacity, but human elevation, as though she needed a stone to keep her where she was. All of her lines were upward and fluted—only her blonde hair, pluming downward, let fall the arc of her exuberant light as it returned to earth.

As I brought her back to my circumference, she responded with complete candor, talking eagerly as though there were no mental stoppage in her anywhere.

"I think I'd better tell you my real name," she began. "It's Margaret, not Margot, Anthony. The Margot is just for the billing. It sounds phony, doesn't it? But my agent insisted, and I gave in. So I'm stuck with it, I guess."

"Let's say that it has a good ring for the theatre," I said, trying to twinkle. "How did it all come about—Rio, I mean? How did you ever get down here?" This one, I said to myself, usually opens the dam.

"Partly for the job," she said directly. "Partly for other reasons. I was getting in a rut. I wasn't getting anywhere in New York. It was too routine. I was simply whirling around on the stage, that's all. I just had to get out of that city. But don't get me wrong." She turned to me impulsively. "I love New York. It was my fault really."

10

"So you turned south for adventure?" I asked, smiling. "I rather thought you might be a bird of passage."

"Now you're teasing me," she said with a laugh. "No, I did not really come down here on a man-hunt, not even for the money—they don't pay that well." She paused. "I know this sounds silly, but I wanted to get away. I had begun to worry about myself."

"Don't tell me there is an 'abyss,'" I said with a look of mock consternation, though the old role of my sardonic patronage seemed a paltry pose with her. "Really, my dear, you will destroy my faith in my 'system' if you don't watch out. You know there is one. I've already put you aside as one of nature's wholly annealed, not subject to fissure."

"There you go again," she said. "I knew you would but I don't mind. Still, it's true. I had to get away."

"But why Rio? Why Brazil, of all places? Surely you didn't need so total an escape." I looked around as though I felt the breath of the jungle at our back.

"Yes, I did," she said without hesitation. "Let me explain— I love dancing, I think you can see that. And I like myself well enough; I've always thought that necessary. And I like the world around me too, the World with a capital letter. But that's all."

"My dear girl, what more in heaven's name do you ask? Isn't that really quite enough? I wish I could say as much."

"No, it isn't enough. Don't you see? That leaves out people. I found out they annoyed me, that they got in my way, that I didn't really like them. And it was beginning to show up in my work—there was nothing there but mechanics, human mechanics. I am what they call a faultless dancer, you know. I never make a mistake. But all I had become was a cylinder of motion."

"And what, may I ask, has all of this got to do with Brazil?" This young woman, I thought, was getting away from me.

"It does sound sort of involved," she admitted, taking a sip of tea and a bite of brioche. When her mood seemed to have found a resting place, she continued slowly. "And it is. You see, I wanted to know people better. It's so hard in New York,

11

don't you think? Everyone's so masterful there. You have to listen mighty hard beneath the rumble to hear the sound of what they're really like. That's why I came to Brazil. Nothing's settled down here; everything is yet to be done. There are not many successes. I suppose you could say I wanted to know some people who were at the mercy of things."

"Well, well, well," I said. "That, at least, is a point of view." I didn't want to sound too interested, for it might close her up with self-consciousness. But, clap hands, I said to myself, here, at last, is an "original."

"You know," she said roguishly, "we're alike. I have a 'system' too, though it's a system that in a way defeats itself. Whenever I meet anyone now, they become a part of my system instead of some property that's cluttering up my stage. I look at them physically first—that's very important. How can they inhabit this particular body, I ask. What is it to be ugly, to be deformed; what is it also to be beautiful—can that be another type of burden—could it be a limitation? I think of what it is to live in the given, not the asked for. And then there are the positions we occupy—some call it 'the cage we live in.' Well, some of us feel like birds there and some of us feel like monkeys. There are so many different places in which a man tries to breathe. The thrill is in seeing the adaptation. You know what Whitman said, 'I am the man, I suffered, I was there.' That's what I want to understand about people, the passionate, ultimate test of their living. When you know the problem involved in being that other person beside you, there are not too many things you can say for sure, though there are some." She leaned over and curved her final words around me as though perhaps she had been too far away. "You see? Didn't I tell you? The system is in not having one."

"And I suppose by this method you have *really* come to like Brazilians? My dear, you haven't gone into some terrible sisterly clutch with them, have you?" I knew I was being sarcastic, and I knew that she would never take it so.

"Of course," she said. "They've been perfectly wonderful to

12

me. They kid me at the *pension* where I live and tell me I'm a *Carioca da gema*. That sort of takes me into all the clubs at once. I even have a boy friend, a real one," she said confidingly. "I never had time in New York. Antonio Sampaio is his name. We see each other every day. He's a dancer at the Urca, not a very good one, but he doesn't mind. He just likes to dance. He's not very good at anything, but he's simply a grand guy."

"This is the rarest recommendation of love I've ever heard," I said, and I let my good humor break through in a laugh. "And how does all this say, 'On with the dance!'?"

"Oh, but it does. Don't you see? It makes all the difference. There's more than a reason now; there's how I feel—like dancing," she said gaily. "Do you know the old French proverb which goes, 'That which cannot be spoken must be sung, that which cannot be sung must be danced'? Well, I've always wanted to feel that way about it, and now I do. We've got lots of plans, Antonio and I. We're going back to the States together. He thinks he would like to manage me instead of dance. And I," she finished with a rippling little laugh, "think he would manage me very well."

She looked out of the window, and I could see that her eyes were filled with the glow of it all. She had got what she had been after. Brazil was her Venus-country—brown and shimmering and utterly lovely, it had loomed up out of her longing, starred with foam, the flesh of love streaming in the liquid aquamarine of southern waters. It had emerged, it would float there forever as the corporeal remembrance of what she had come seeking. Or so she thought, poor dear. Or so she thought. . . . But was it only this? Could it be I who saw the manatee instead of the mermaid? Was it I who lived in a throttled world of vision, eyes bloodshot and nearly blind with the strangling hands of my own denial, while she, this last and most fragile member of my company, had flown in the face of it all and won? It was she who had come across the shining axe which a manic god had driven into the brain of man without sundering it, and, discovering that old wound of dualism and distress, had sought to

13

bind it up. She had learned what is meant by the *whole* body of love. She had refused to accept the cleavage while I, like a surgeon in the face of carnage, had been ruthless and precise as I looked at the ancient, fumbled amputation of the still-unsevered heart and mind. What were all my catalogues, my dichotomies and divisions in the light of her unsutured loveliness?

It was nearly sundown and time for her to go. I took her to the bus stop, holding her hand in good-bye rather longer than I should have, and I wondered what she thought of me (I had given her so little to go on). Perhaps as just another well-heeled, aging American living abroad to avoid the dislocations of war. But no, I had forgotten. That was not her "method."

I put her on the bus and watched its long, lumbering shape, like the gray, battered thorax of a huge, dead insect, merge into the twilight traffic as it foamed down the evening—she had brushed against me and was gone. I felt tired and faint, and, not wanting to return to the apartment with its musty old collection of impaled memories, I shifted around for something to do. I had the longing to be on my way, the desire to be somewhere else—there was a dim, delusive pull of magnetism in my blood. It was this damned, melancholy weather, this autumn that was not autumn, this false October that made one feel foolish and sentimental. What I needed was a change. That was it—a trip! It would have to be somewhere on the continent, though—military priorities would see to that. There was Buenos Aires. No, that would never do. Nor Caracas, nor Santiago. I was tired of them all. They would only depress me. I would be met at the airport by a corps of shadows like so many secret-service men. Then, it would have to be the great cataracts at Iguassú in a southern corner of the Brazilian borderlands. I had been there before, but, no matter, it stirred my appetite more than all the others.

I closed my eyes and listened for the white thunder of the falls as they rushed over the colossal, jutting lip of rock and poured on down the valley. Yes, I could still hear it and see it too. When I had been there before, I had bathed nude in a little,

14

thrillingly cold, whirling basin, just beyond the tremendous drop of the water so that some of the vibration shook through my body as though it threatened my heart. Perhaps I would do that again. But most of all I wanted to see the fabulous butterflies, yellow and brown, tremulous and glistening, clinging to the long, wet grass which hung down from the bank on either side of the channel. When the sun fell upon them, they seemed ignited with a glorious interior-burning and jeweled the great throat of the water, responding to its gigantic arterial throbbing with the pulsation of their wings. Sometimes they rose in a swarm and crossed the fuming cataract, flying so low that the smoke of the spray enveloped them in a thin, womb-like cloud until they emerged in a wing-burst of gold like an exhalation of the violent water.

Yes, perhaps it would be worth it. I wanted to see the falls again. I wanted to stand and watch the trembling of those wings.

A PASSION FOR EMERALDS

M*AIS UM,"* THE BLONDE YOUNG WOMAN SAID LOUD-
ly, shoving her beer mug toward a white-coated boy.

The little café on the first floor of the Metropole steamed
with odors of *comida brasileira,* and it was incongruous to see
almost nothing but Americans shouting bad Portuguese to the
volatile waiters who skittered by. The food was poor but the
beer excellent, and one didn't have to walk out into the summer sun since the Embassy annex was on the floors above.

It was certainly as far as Jim Walker wanted to go with the
blonde who looked as though she would lard the streets of Rio
if he risked taking her through the heat to one of the better
restaurants. The Old Goat had asked him to invite her to lunch
since this was her first morning in the office, and he had had to
comply. He looked at her aloofly, with barely concealed dis-
taste. What in the hell was she doing in Rio anyway? She was
all that he loathed in a woman, big, boisterous, pugnacious-look-
ing. At least five feet nine, she could have run interference on
a football team, her shoulders humped high in a padding of fat.
The arms were particularly repulsive, hanging down large and
meaty from the short sleeves of her summer dress like etiolated
hams.

But it was not only her size that repelled. She was otherwise
outlandish-looking with her hair in bangs like a wig that concealed a balding head and pressed against her ears in weird, flat
braids. Even more annoying was the fact that she was not all of

19

a piece. He couldn't classify her as one more blowzy female on the loose and let it go at that, for there were touches in her dress, moments of decorum in her manner, a kind of glaze of superiority which suggested the lady. Her long, straight nose and short upper lip were patrician, and the blue eyes were those of a Hedda Gabler, arrogant even in laughter. But of one thing there could be no doubt. She was very much *there,* mythically American, conceived in the ponderous image of the Statue of Liberty.

Her prevalence was particularly discomforting, for Walker hated to be conspicuous, the object of even momentary ridicule, and he knew that they were quite a pair together. He was a formalist by nature, and this little scene promised to have all the disorder of "life itself," as people were so fond of saying. At thirty-four he had never married, but his very aloofness, his decontaminated quality, had brought a number of women his way. Lean, trim, and dark, wearing glasses over brown eyes, he was ascetically handsome, without the rich saturation in himself which good-looking men often possess. He and the blonde—incredibly enough, her name was Anna Covington Parker—were the "bones and flesh" of life, and it was the way she swelled dangerously near him and, by projection, around him, that he resented most. There she was on her third beer and the fruit cup not even finished! She must store it in her arms, he thought gruesomely.

When the boy set down her mug, she looked at it glowing in the sun like a chalice of her pleasure and said with obnoxious good spirits, "Well, this is the life, eh what, Mr. Walker? We couldn't do this back home, could we? Take an hour and a half and get looping at lunch. That's what I like about the tropics, the abandon. Nobody gives a damn."

"Really," he said dourly. Yes, she *was* going to be a trial. No wonder they had tossed her into Agriculture. He had heard by the grapevine that she had made them all sigh frostily over in Chancellery, and they had not quite known what to do with her.

Someone had been requested for Cultural Relations, but who would have thought that State, hard up as it was for wartime personnel, would have sent down a Carnival queen. But she was to be kept in Rio rather than exiled to the provinces along with the other "accidents" the Department had made. In her case, there were connections. He remembered the piecemeal rumors now: two parents in *Who's Who,* a prominent Washington family, auras of the horsey crowd, a country place in Virginia. And she *was* a *cum laude* from Smith. That he knew from her papers.

"Yes," she went on, raising her mug, jangling a bracelet of heavy costume gold and green stones. "I simply decided it had to be Rio, and here I am. *Saúde!*" The toast came out like a burp, and Walker cringed, but she continued with opulent fluency. "I wish you'd tell me something about our work before we go back upstairs. You know, I don't know a damn thing about Agriculture. I came down for Cultural Relations, but there was a mix-up in my orders, I believe. I suppose you know I'm Administrative Assistant to Mr. Brown. Tell me, what's he like? Is he hard to get along with?"

This was incredible, Walker thought; she was already treating him like a confederate, an equal. It took the strong memory of the fact that he was Third Secretary and Vice-Consul and that she was only an aberration in the disordered soul of the Department to keep him in balance. Anyway, he could leave her to the Old Goat who was an intruder too, one of the Department's wartime collection, for it always took one to kill one. It would be fun to watch the fireworks, and, in answer to her question, he cleverly laid stepping stones that led straight into a bog, taking care that she would never be able to remember how she was sent astray. He made it sound like a honeymoon for a young lady who was not afraid to speak her mind, and she bubbled gratefully, calling for another beer, "a little sedative for the afternoon."

When lunch was over she had tossed her life to him in large chunks, and he was left not quite buried alive, grunting an

21

occasional "Yes. No. Is that so?" It seemed that preparations for her job had been on an invasive scale. She had gone to see everybody who was anybody in Washington for briefing on the intricacies of diplomacy, and had enrolled in the Harvard Summer School for an intensive course in Portuguese until she could spit it out like glass in the mouth.

"If they think I'm going to be just a little ole secretary down here, they're crazy. You know, I can't even type, so I'll just have to work on policy and administration, won't I?" She winked wickedly. "Get it? Play dumb and let someone else push the wagon."

The rest of the afternoon was spent on Anna's settling in. Back in his office, Walker felt her presence throbbing against the walls portentously, and it appalled him that perhaps they would never seem strong enough again. And yet he could not resist opening the door to catch glimpses of her poking around into everything, "casing the joint." The secretary, Sally Montgomery, who had never been known to speak above a whisper, was letting out loose, nervous, little plumes of laughter, regaled with a retelling of the "story." But an imperial flourish came at the end when Anna laid down her rights.

"I see we're missing a secretary, Sally." She glanced at the vacant desk. "We'll simply have to get someone else. You know I'm not an office girl, and you won't be able to handle my work as well as Brown's and Walker's. You see, I'm Brown's new assistant. I suppose I really should have a desk in his office." She looked around as though various ideas about the furniture had occurred to her.

Walker listened with a mounting, heady mixture of anger and pleasure, for he knew the break would come soon. He experienced a real catharsis when the Old Goat trotted out, scowling truculently, fanning the smell of stale beer from his nose. Sixtyish, dumpy, not over five feet three, brown as an earth-clod, he had a sour face which said that everything insulted him. Vindictive little animal eyes peered through steel-rimmed

22

glasses, and his white moustache over curling lips gave him a goatish look. Walker hated the "old shoe," his lack of class, his soul of a mean little bully, but, for the moment, felt a perverse glow of warmth for him.

"Miss Montgomery," he said curtly. "Come into my office please. I want you to take some dictation." He looked at Anna without a trace of courtesy. "And, Miss Parker, you might spend the afternoon going over the files getting acquainted with our work. Come in first thing in the morning, and I'll tell you what your duties are. We start at nine o'clock sharp, you know."

Walker could see them eying each other, the terrible pigmy and the tawny Amazon. Anna took a deep breath as though she could blow him out of the world if she would and said, "Yes, sir," but her submission was ominous, the pause of a hand above a crawling fly.

Next morning, Walker had already conferred with Brown about the work of the day, taking occasion to prod him in just the right places about the new arrival, when Anna stalked in fifteen minutes late grumbling about "the damn Brazilian buses. You'd think they were taking you on a tour of the city." On his way out, he smiled darkly at her. "He's all yours, Miss Parker."

"Oh, come on, wish me luck, Walker. Anybody would think you're scared of him," she whispered impudently as she surged past, crowding him against the wall.

He would have liked to slap her face, for the morning already had a pleasant sadistic tingle about it. And he would have given a month's salary to be in on the showdown. It was downright disheartening that there was no shouting, no hunks of hair or a few stray false teeth heaved through the door. But when Anna returned, "full" was the word for her, frazzled but grander than ever, a consort for Lucifer. She sat down at the other secretarial desk, tucked her voluminous handbag carefully into a drawer as though it contained dynamite, folded her arms and peered down at the blotter like an empty map whose strategy would be staked out with human heads.

23

One afternoon six months later, Walker sat alone in his office, given over to the inertia of the languorous day, waiting for Miss Parker to come in and arouse him with some unexpected irritation. Yes, she had become a sort of drug; he needed her to get the day started. Sally was no good, she never did anything wrong, and the Old Goat was tiresomely predictable. But Anna's capacity for taking issue was endless without becoming repetitious. She had become the great golden gadfly of his Southern slumber.

Why didn't she come in, he wondered, so that he could toss her out and settle down to an active tranquillity? Though the door to the reception room was closed, he could hear the muted torrent of her life tumbling through the morning air. Giddy girandoles of laughter rose above the grand current of her voice—that would be some of the retainers, of course. She was holding court and getting away with it as usual.

Looking back over the past months, Walker realized that he had been contending with a way of life subversive to his own. Though forced to act as secretary, Anna had made this the chief function of the office. Her desk was inlet and outlet for the tides of their activity. The files had been completely reorganized according to a system understood best by her but apparently representing a terrific new aspect of efficiency. No one could get in to see him or Mr. Brown without preliminary screening, for she believed in the presenting of credentials. There was no such thing any more as a personal letter or private phone call. Correspondence with a distinctly unofficial look somehow got "opened by mistake," and anyone who telephoned was asked to state his business. But, in spite of the valvular control, a spring freshet of work poured out of the office. Anna discovered a miraculous ability to type at a rapid speed, and Agricultural reports that had lain festering for months were made ready. Though she was intermittently an enormous lounger, when the mood was right she could pound the typewriter mercilessly as though it were the only enemy.

24

The Old Goat had long since capitulated, only trotting out occasionally to look around as if escape might one day be possible, grunting some command which would be carried out according to Anna's whim as to whether "it was the right thing to do." Of late, she had taken more and more to going over his head, asking Walker to initial the dispatches when she came back to discuss "policy" with him, intimating that if he were half a man, he would have had the Old Goat's job a long time ago.

For she loved nothing better, Walker had learned, than invading his privacy, taking every occasion to barge in unexpectedly until he felt rather like the adolescent boy whose mother twitched the covers off when he lay too long abed. She knew if she made him mad enough, he would think up something really "super" for her to do, and that would start another disputatious round. There was a quality in his scorn, Walker concluded, which fascinated her. He overheard her tell a crony, "That Walker's a real s.o.b. But I'm wearing him down. He's my little insoluble. Maybe someday I'll give up and toss him in the rock crusher." And she made a grinding noise with her teeth.

But the greatest change Anna had brought about was not in others but in herself, as though so definite a type had to be crossed with its opposite, longing for ascendancy. Physically she looked so different that she almost should have had a new name. The blonde hair now fell to her shoulders sinuously, only the bangs remaining, forming an airy, yellow cowl around her stark white face which was marked with deep circles under the eyes like smudges made by heavy, black fingers. A rigid diet had left nothing but the gaunt framework of her energy and still she continued to lose weight with a discipline almost sensual. Though the days of stale beer on the breath were gone, the boundlessness in her temperament was transformed, not dead. She boasted loudly about her gambling sprees at the casino, sometimes flashing a role of *cruzeiros* like a withered corsage of her winnings. Her eyes rolled in the manner of blue disks in a

25

celluloid toy when she bragged about her prowess with the samba, and Walker shuddered at the thought of her large skeleton aloft, bumping and rattling around as though it needed the remembered ballast of obesity.

Nothing but "love" could have brought on a reformation so dolefully buoyant, Walker reflected, to whom the cause and the effect seemed of doubtful rational cohesion. The lover-boy was a young Navy lieutenant, Payson Chandler, something of a pansy Walker had always thought, whom Anna hung over her arm as easily as a scarf the first time she saw him despite her vociferous hostility to this species of male, having often hinted balefully that the Embassy was nothing but a "house"—"You know what I mean, Mr. Walker. A real *house*. It's a disgrace. They should know about it back home. Take that Mr. Hall. He ought to be named Radclyffe. Have you ever seen the way he walks—if you can call it that? And that Peterson ghoul. If he ever came out from behind those dark glasses and took a look at the world, he'd faint."

But Payson when he was off duty could wear neckties as gaudy as a peasant skirt and Anna staunchly defended his manhood like a possession he had given her to keep. Of course, she was making a fool of herself. But let her. One day he would find a way of taking the top of her head off, and she wouldn't know it until later when she felt the draft in her brains.

If he had believed in Nemesis, Walker would have recollected later how violently the seasoned bitterness of his thoughts was broken off while he sat there chewing his cud of "Annarisms." As he described it later, he was enveloped in a loud explosion, went "up and then down" like a man shot through a cannon, dropping without transition in a parachute to fall and stop with a jolt, held fast in the harness at the end of the rope which in the rapid synaesthesia of the moment melded and solidified and "became" his swivel chair.

Anna ran in as though drawn by the suction of his fall.

"Oh, Mr. Walker, did you call?" she said, and even at that

moment of dispersal Walker was delighted with the supreme fatuousness of her remark.

"Yes, Miss Parker. I *think* I did," he gasped. "I'm over here. *Not* on the ceiling. You can come over. I'm not radioactive." He lay quietly in the uncomfortable peril of the chair, now become a wooden crotch, his feet dangling, his head hung back in decapitated limpness, for he wanted her to see him *in situ.*

"Dear me, Mr. Walker—the chair—it exploded, didn't it?"

"Yes, I believe it did, Miss Parker. Everything I am tells me that it is so." He looked up as though an eye, an arm, a soul, might still fall in place and complete his recognition.

The Old Goat ran down the hall, puffing from trying to get there in time.

"Walker, are you all right? What the hell's going on down here anyway? You weren't doing *jiu jitsu* with Miss Parker, I hope." He leered wickedly and grabbed at the end of his moustache as though he pulled the bell-rope of his vindictive good humor.

Anna moved quickly toward him, using her body like a door.

"It's nothing at all, Mr. Brown. There's been a little accident. Mr. Walker's had a shock, and I think we'd better not crowd him. I'll see to it. You don't need to worry." She had the air now of one experienced with earthquakes and the Old Goat stepped back heavily onto the foot of Sally who loomed anxiously near, and, when she squealed, there was a siphon in the confusion which left Anna alone with the "victim."

As the door closed, Anna breathed deeply of command and came toward Walker in whom curiosity and indignation violently contended, but he lay there waiting. She bent over him for a moment and there was the strength of the curve of the sky in her back, and he realized that it was the only still moment that had ever existed between them. There was a curious nuance of grief in it, the shadow of the capaciousness which her body had lost came back like a memory of what use it had longed to put itself, and he could have sworn she wanted to kiss him.

Then bringing back motion, she fluttered like a great, golden bird ready to take him to the Elysian fields, a superior world, a substitute existence.

Anger rose in him, but fell back weakly, a geyser diminishing into itself. That moment which stretched to the far corners of their acquaintance and blotted out all of the rest, returning to the center like spreading circles in a playback of reality, had seen him "broken." He felt as though one of his most important personal traits had been sundered, his courage or reserve, and the fluid of sarcasm drained slowly from his veins. Above this ruin an atmosphere of mammoth tenderness hovered which threatened to suffocate him, and he was thankful when Anna, like a ventriloquist casting the old familiar voice into a body which had now become strange to him, spoke out brashly and cheerily as she helped him out of the tilted chair.

"Never say die, say damn, Mr. Walker." She picked up his glasses which were broken at the bridge and pretended to dust and straighten his suit.

"That God-damned chair!" he complied at last, breaking the trance. "I thought a terrorist had gotten me." Gutty feelings flooded back, feeding his dry surprise like a red river. "Are you sure you didn't come in the dark of night and tamper with that mainspring, Miss Parker?" Something about the way she had touched him just now had snapped him out of it. He recalled the other meaning of that moment of the hovering kiss, and it now seemed gustatory, as though she had come upon the only forbidden morsel in an edible world.

"I sure did, Mr. Walker. I'd work nights for a month just to see you bend in the middle," she said.

"You probably would, Miss Parker. You probably would." His nearsighted eyes strained in the haze to form a cutting edge.

"You sure were a pretty sight. Lucky you didn't bump your head. Some people are never the same afterwards."

"Do you speak from experience?" he asked demurely.

"Oh, no, Mr. Walker. I'm just the way God made me. Never had an accident or a sickness in my life."

28

"You mean you're one of those who just kept growing merrily along?"

"That's right. Papa says when I was a little girl he used to wonder if I'd ever wake up tired."

"Did your father die a long time ago?"

She looked at him and laughed raucously. "Why, Mr. Walker, you do say the funniest things. You know, you're getting to be downright witty. It must have been that jolt. I told you you'd never be the same." She picked up something from the table. "I feel so good I think I'll knock off and fix your glasses. You didn't know I was a mechanic at heart, did you?"

"No, that hadn't come to me yet."

"Well, I am. I just hate to type. Give me a machine shop any day. I can fix anything in a jiffy. Did you ever hear that song, 'I'm just a Kitchen Mechanic,' dum de dum, dum, dum?" She rolled her eyes and thumped the desk.

The dwindling afternoon was spent on patching his glasses with adhesive tape and attempting to repair the swivel chair which Anna picked up like a toy, reattaching, to her own satisfaction, the broken spring, though Walker advised her to tack on a sign, "Explosive, Handle With Care." He had never seen her in better spirits. She hummed, buzzed, and wisecracked while he thumbed at his dispatches blindly, feeling her life shimmying the room like a generator. In the old-fashioned phrase, she seemed to be happiest "doing" for him, and the whole thing had a steamy domestic atmosphere like a laundry or a nursery after the baby's bath. But Parker didn't really like him, he knew; she merely wanted to catch him "naked"—she was after the primordial child. It was merely another way of destroying the male at the bare, post-foetal stage of it all.

At least that was still as positive as he could be about that sulphurous miasma which she called a soul, for, in spite of all her sharp, particular, apparently characteristic acts, she was still diffuse to him. He had a habit privately of thinking of people in terms of animals or things—Mr. Brown could be dismissed as the Old Goat and Sally conceived of caressively as a dear

29

little rabbit. But Anna was amorphous—a golden cloud, a blonde pervasiveness darkening at times to threat of storm. She was one of those people who seem to want to remind one of something, somewhere else. Now he realized that he had been taking in great draughts of her for months, his nostrils wide open, as through scent we gather together memory into a form, some aroma of personality that promises to belong to memory. If he had liked her better, he would have said that perhaps she reminded him of home, impregnating the foreign air with American allusiveness, streaking it with the rich currents of another climate.

After the "debacle of the chair," as Walker privately referred to it, Anna's personality began to pile up before him in a precarious, nearly zigzag heap like boxes set sloppily one on the other, and the hand, from a generalized human desire to see a fall, longed to give it a shove. As the work in the office settled down into humdrum routine, she compensated with her most extravagant behavior, giving herself a "bounce" by blowing in most of her salary on jewelry at Hugo's. She had already acquired a large aquamarine, a topaz, an amethyst, and "several little trinkets" from Payson. No man was a sport who saved his money, and Walker decided her tropic proliferation was complete when she discussed what he called her "gemcrack" phase with him.

"You know, Walker, jewels have a life all their own. Take a guy that doesn't know that, a real tightwad, I mean. Well, you'll find he doesn't know anything else worth knowing either."

But it was to Dr. Edgar Babcock that she philosophized most precisely on this subject. Babcock, an agronomy expert from the University of Missouri lent to the Brazilian Government for consultation, had fallen willingly into her toils when he first entered the office. A bachelor of fifty, a prissy but pleasant man, good-hearted and intelligent, he was thoroughly susceptible to the "great girl" such as she. He adored her, and she had his life in Rio organized for him almost the day he arrived. But he liked Walker too, thought him a decent fellow, brainier than

30

the average career man, and they had become rather clubbily intimate. Anna, determined not to be excluded, played one against the other mercilessly. Babcock found her vastly amusing, gave up sightseeing time in order to loaf around her in the office, and she knew her man, assaulting his dignity in just the places he secretly wanted it to be piqued until he was always in a pleasurable dither. With Walker and Sally she called him "Babzinho," her own version of the Portuguese diminutive of his name, and once on a sleepy afternoon did a "female" impersonation of him singing "Violate me in violet time in the vilest way that you know," which was riotous and yet made him somehow more endearing.

A few days before Babcock returned to the States, Anna was advising him on what to take back. "Jewels, Dr. Babcock, I assure you, jewels. There's nothing else worth while. There's no art down here, I suppose you know that. Not an author you'd ever want to read when you got back home. But jewels, yes, they do have jewels."

Mr. Brown called Walker into his office, but he felt like crowing with delight for he knew the two sides of that discussion would converge toward him in the end. A half hour later he was sitting complacently in his chair waiting when Babcock entered, looking somewhat drained as by some heroic action but chuckling pleasantly.

"Jim, I suppose you heard. Anna's been after me about the jewels."

"Yes, I know. I hope you sent her packing."

"Well, no, not exactly. She wanted me to buy an aquamarine for my sister. I told her that wasn't quite good enough. I thought I'd get an emerald."

"What!"

"Yes, I know that sounds crazy. But it just popped into my head like the natural thing to say. I think it gave her quite a shock."

"Well, I'm sure it did. I'm surprised she didn't sprout a dozen arms and strangle you with love."

31

"She did get red in the face. Sort of like somebody had opened up a big furnace door."

"You're not going through with it, of course—just because that big blonde bully made you say something foolish. Emeralds, my God, man!"

"No." Dr. Babcock squirmed uneasily. "I haven't got that kind of money. But I can't say I'm sorry," he continued reflectively. "I think it did give her quite a thrill."

"Naturally, but that's beside the point. You don't know what you're in for. She'll track you down. She'll make you *show* the bill of sale and what's more the emerald."

"No, I got around that. I told her I was picking it up just before I left. And, you know, the funny thing is, she believed me."

"But why did you do it at all? In heaven's name why?"

"I don't know. I just suddenly said it. I knew she would like it. And it seemed like a good thing to say." He looked up almost pleadingly. "I suppose you think I'm an awful fool."

"Well, Babcock, I can't say this is the most brilliant move you ever made," Walker said, trying hard to keep from laughing.

"I guess I was thinking about Anna, the way she takes things. Maybe I can explain it this way—did you ever run across that tale about Mount Kâf, the mountain grounded in emerald which Mohammedans believe encircles the earth? Well, Anna is sort of like that. She wants to think the whole world is built on a jewel. Let her believe that, Walker, and she'll let you alone. She knows most of us think it's all basalt. That's why she's after us." He paused, and his eyes looked dim as gray stones under water. "I suppose it's hard to try to be happy, maybe harder than being . . . well . . . like us."

Walker would have answered—there was surely a slope on the other side which could lead them down into their usual rapport, but Babcock forgot for once to level off. He merely stepped abruptly through the door's precipitous edge as if a fall would do him good. There was hardly time for the little slamming concussion to stop reverberating like an after-crash when Anna came through the side entrance.

"Walker," she said. "Hold me up. I need help. Don't refuse me just this once." She leaned against the desk and her smile was nearly iridescent with mingling feelings. "The old boy's gone and done it. He's shot the works. Isn't he the most adorable man you've ever known?"

"Parker," he said, forgetting the *Miss* for the first time. "Control yourself. What on earth are you carrying on about?"

"Babzinho—" Suddenly her confidence had never been more radiant. "Of course. I had forgotten. Naturally he wouldn't tell you first. He wanted me to do that." She leaned forward with a great, luscious air of conspiracy that threatened to encircle Walker like a golden arm.

"What makes you so sure?" he asked, feeling a throbbing fist of venom in his mind.

"You could never guess. He would never tell, I see that now," she went on devotedly, though Walker sat as impassive as an idol. "I had to worm it out of him myself. He's so shy, you know, such a darling. But it's true. He's simply doing a grand thing. He's buying an emerald for his sister, a big one. She's an old maid, you know. They live together."

She tossed her hair back and gave him a long, arching look like a curve of her world let down behind him. "Walker, I'd give a thousand dollars to be that woman when he gives her that gorgeous green rock."

Walker felt it coming now, and he could have wished that some great hand would stanch his mouth, for all the realm of counter-possibility, full of beckoning, luminous shapes, bulged against the membrane of the moment.

"You don't believe he will do it, do you?" he asked tonelessly as though it were better to sound like someone else.

"What do you mean? Of course, I do. After all, I'm the one who put him up to it. And all the time I thought he was a cheapskate."

Then she began to notice his face, the one, he thought to himself, she couldn't control.

"You haven't talked to him, have you? You didn't persuade him not to do it? It's not a trick. It's on the level, isn't it?" Her face flickered with a tinge of Plutonian darkness, and Walker glanced down at his desk.

"Don't be absurd, Anna. Really, old girl, why don't you grow up?"

When he did not hear her familiar, raucous laughter, he looked up with his most sardonic smile, certain that it would bring on a swift reprisal. But she waited there gauntly, almost as though listening for echoes of her old flamboyance to prompt her, gripped with the obsession in his face that she should rise to the occasion. As he stood up at last in the overpowering quiet, he felt harder and taller than ever before, a dark pillar to whom the only person alive had somehow tied herself. But still she didn't move, very white now, the gold and green bracelet hung sprawling on her arm like bruises from a twisting chain. There was a quality of lost music about it all, and the walls of the room wanted to yield and melt to a film of gauze beyond which shimmered the reversal of pillar and suppliant. It was she who looked like a columnar statue, glorious in a green world of spring, with him in attendance, and the depth of his life seemed yearningly close.

34

THE MOTION OF
FORGETFULNESS IS SLOW

THEY MET AT THE ATLANTICO, ONE OF RIO'S MOST popular nightclubs. They knew from the beginning why they were sitting next to each other, and this enabled them to dispense with the stiff and tedious preliminaries of conversation and be almost immediately easy and informal. Their hostess, Jacqueline Laurent, was a garrulous, masculine, French woman of forty-five, a refugee, somewhat bitter about life, but still a great arranger of romance, an authority on the principles of love, although she had no lover at the moment, and it was doubtful whether she would ever have one again. Some said she was a Lesbian, but that was probably untrue since it would have been too easy and almost natural for her, and she was a woman who enjoyed what was most difficult for her to do. Her preoccupation with love had made her widely and ardently social, and she was a familiar figure of café society. Though people feared her, knowing that she could be vicious or benevolent according to whim, they were always glad to be entertained by her because she was never dull. With her penchant for intrigue, she never gave a party that did not have its implications of the destruction or arousal of a liaison between at least one of the couples present.

She had chosen the proper time for this particular conspiracy. A few weeks later, and it might never have happened. But, tonight, success was probable. She knew it, they knew it, and, as a consequence, the surface of the evening moved rapidly. Since

37

she liked them both so well, she had gone to some trouble to inform and prepare them carefully beforehand so that nothing would go amiss. Ingrid Lombard was an old friend from the prewar days in Paris, and Robert Atherton, a young journalist with the Office of the Coordinator of Inter-American Affairs, had won her sympathy not only through his personal charm but because he was a type which she liked, very blondly and brightly American, evoking sentimental memories of her life in the United States when she toured the country on the old Keith vaudeville circuit singing French songs.

Jacqueline knew, and she was satisfied now that they knew, what she called the "circumstances." A week before, Ingrid's husband, Monsieur Charles Lombard, had left for Paris, recently occupied by the American army, and it was understood that he would not return. Monsieur Lombard was a handsome man of fifty, a painter of minor talent but much ego, possessed of the aloofness and confidence that are often so attractive to women. Ingrid had met him ten years before when she came from Sweden to study art in France. Out of her respect and need for love she had made of him something he was not, but something she could admire, and they lived rather happily together until his selfish possession of her was sated. Now at thirty-nine it was hard for her to lose him, and for the moment she had almost ceased to exist since she realized that the world of her invention, of which he was the center, had really never had any validity at all. There is nothing lonelier than living among the ruins of belief, and because she could not bear this loneliness she had come to Jacqueline's party.

Robert Atherton had not known much about love when he came to Brazil. Like many young Americans of thirty, he had slept with a girl or two, but the relationship had always been of short duration, rather frantically and hectically physical—the kind of experience that later enabled him to understand what a Brazilian friend meant when he said that love in America was usually a matter of athletics. The girls he had known at the University had been wholesome, usual in opinion and attitude, pretty but sexually rather dull, and he had lost interest in them quickly. Not long after his arrival in Brazil, he met Yvonne Vautier, who had come to Rio to visit friends and had been stranded there by the outbreak of war. She was urban in manner and outlook, small, unathletic, but firm and trim of figure, and she had a very intense color of red-gold hair and brilliant blue eyes. She was two years older than he, had been married once and in love several times. She liked Robert, understood him quickly, and became his mistress after six weeks. They had a *garçonnière* together, and Robert went through a complete experience of love, beyond the merely sensual, beyond the spirit of youthful adventure, and knew for the first time what Europeans meant by falling in love mentally as well as physically. Jacqueline, who was a close friend of Yvonne, had enjoyed every stage of the affair, thinking it a perfect union of the Old World—New World. She foresaw what would happen to Robert when Yvonne found it necessary to return to her family in Paris, was ready with comfort after the departure and, finally, the party and the meeting with Ingrid.

They knew, and yet they had come, were staying, and were going through with it. They knew it was one of Jacqueline's little amusements, and that it might be desperate for them, but there was a chance it might not be, and nothing was worse than shutting the door completely and admitting it was over, that one had been loved and now was not loved and might not love again since love was miraculous and even haphazard and accidental and not to be expected more than once in a lifetime. No, it was better to pretend that the door was still open in a place where self-deception was possible, where there were people, music, and motion—pretend, at least for tonight, that circumstances were still fluid, that it should and would happen again, that it might happen more beautifully than before.

The party of six couples, all foreigners, was masterfully engineered by Jacqueline, although she was not really interested in any of them except Ingrid and Robert who were the nerves in the body of the group. It was their presence alone that excited

39

and stimulated her and enabled her to play with skill the part of the gracious hostess, knowing that the whole elaborate social texture of eating and drinking, gestures and small talk, had a purpose and a center of intensity, a covert drama which was of her own instigation. As they talked, they were conscious of the fact that through the sound and actions of others present, in intrusions and withdrawals, the unpredictable pattern and direction of reciprocal speech, the sudden close-knit vocal una-nimity, Jacqueline was listening to them with a focus of atten-tion, central and direct beneath its superficial digressiveness.

They knew that they were being used, and they did not care. They knew that Jacqueline was increasing the sense of her own power by finding them, for the moment at least, pliant in her hands. If things worked out as she intended, she would never let them forget. No, she would never let go of them. But sometimes it is better to be used than to remain inert since movement is life, and in both of them there had been a great and sudden slowing down, so that memory receded into the past hardly at all and the present was stagnant as if the means of extending feeling had been shut off within the blood, leaving in the heart neither the possibility of death nor birth. Jacqueline promised to unlock this rigidity. So being used was moving and better than being still at the point where one could not move volun-tarily, the point where someone outside had to play Fate and free the congealing of circumstance.

Inside where there were music and light, and whisky had loosened the tightness of thought, it was possible to feel the surface of life moving, not quickly yet, but mobile again and moving toward the old rapidity. It was possible to believe this even more securely, knowing that Jacqueline was helping it happen. Jacqueline, too, from the outside believed, and it is the viewpoint beyond the personal which supports confidence. Yes, she was very sure. When they left at midnight, their sense of identity which had been hard and stopped was fluid again, lightened and diluted in the hazy but swirling suspension which alcohol makes in the mind. The past did not weigh as much as

40

it had, so that they felt they could move through it or around it and that it was not any more oneself lying in a closed small place. And Jacqueline was standing there, telling them good-bye, sure of it, smiling and solicitous like an accomplice. The last thing they saw was her mouth with the thick, coarse lips, smiling and obscene in the foreground, and if it had not been for the whisky they would have been embarrassed.

Then in the cab they were not so sure of motion, although the physical movement was there in the rolling of the wheels along the Avenida Atlantica, down the damp curve of the beach in the phantom-dim light. Through the open windows the rawness of the sea came in. The apartment houses were all dark and like a huge cliff on one side, and there was a heaviness again everywhere. By contrast, the sea was loose and flatulent, having no thrust and incisiveness where it struck the ponderous earth, pouring on the sand a white spray without power. They said nothing and sat apart, strange and stiff, on either side of the seat. It was not a long drive, but it felt long and stretched out as though the pace of the moments had shifted again and was going slower and might stop altogether. The driver sat at the wheel, rigid, tense, noncommunicative, strangely so for a member of his trade, and seemed to lean with intensity on the accelerator like a man who kept his feelings distended in order that they might remain fluent at all in a night of thickening dross.

Ingrid had an apartment in the hills above the city. Most of the foreigners lived there because of the long open view of the sea, the lighter air, and the feeling of being above the tropic languor of the beaches. But tonight the fog and sea-mist were reaching up into the higher air and were curdling around the tops of the hills, and it was hard to imagine that morning would ever open the sky again and that the harbor would lie there below in a rippling scarf of blue, fluid with outward-going ships and racing light.

When the car stopped at the top of the hill before the entrance to the apartment, laboriously and massively as though the functions of the engine had finally been choked with night,

41

Ingrid said to Robert quietly, "Come in. Come in and have a drink."

"All right," he said, and they went into the dark entrance without looking to see whether the cab moved on.

Inside it was better, with the rawness of the damp air leaving their skin and the warm interior light, and they could forget a little the strange solidification of the drive up the hills away from the music and movement of the nightclub and Jacqueline, glowing, triumphant, transmitting impulse and impulse as though her body were the channel for the current. But now it was better again, although the house was not cheerful. It was furnished as a foreigner might furnish a house, thinking of home. There were things that recalled Sweden and Paris, and they looked dead and rootless here, as they would have in any of the fashionable apartments of the city where one always sensed beneath the structure of modernity the jungle earth, unreceptive to anything that was superimposed and not of its own. But more than this, the living room where they were sitting was cheerless because of the things that were missing, little things that had indicated that two were living there, closely and intimately, and whose absence now said one, and one alone, one, now and perhaps forever, alone.

She had nothing in the house but gin, and it was bad to mix it with the whisky, but there had to be somewhere to start from and this was not like the nightclub at all but a sliding backward to a point where the emotions were once more constricted, and they would not have been able to start again without something to drink. But as the gin awakened the ebbing, warm radiance in their bodies, they wanted to talk and to knit the nightclub feeling and the feeling of now together. And he began to see her for the first time through his own eyes, not remembering very much of what Jacqueline had told him to think, and he wondered whether she were seeing him similarly.

The reddish hair and the blue eyes, he was thinking. *Like Yvonne, and yet not like her, not like her at all. The red hair and blue eyes of Sweden. Not Paris. No, not from Paris. Not*

42

delicate and very slender-compact. Not small of shoulder and
breast. Not the small mouth and the blue eyes with a film of the
sea across them. But very kind and generous like her body, fill-
ing the sofa with abundance and the wish to give it and the feel-
ing that her abundance lies fallow and unclaimed.

And now, perhaps she was thinking—still remembering partly
what Jacqueline had said, not being able to forget the other one
wholly—*he is thinking of her. And is needing not to think of*
her, not to remember because it hurts, but to touch and be
touched, finding the under-depth and the inner, healing, pain-
forgetting heart of touch. Wanting to forget, being young, and
not yet all-despairing. Remembering and not wanting to remem-
ber how love suffers. But remembering and still remembering.
Being young, uncynical, and what I would have wanted of love.

Then they were speaking aloud, but it was difficult, for Jacqueline was not there, transmitting impulse and impulse, joining their diffidence through the force and confidence of her personality. It was difficult because there was a feeling of guilt
beneath their being together. A feeling of betrayal and shame at
trying to forget too soon, and yet, undyingly, the wanting and
willingness to love, the furtive hope of filling the image in the
heart with another image, of blending form, gesture, and word
upon the memory of another form, other gestures, words that
were now a consummation and a death, inert and final, forcing
upon the mind the recognition of not-love, the fear, hardest to
bear, that love lies in a compartment of the soul severed from
current consciousness, suspended and immobile in the enslave-
ment of memory.

The music of the samba came in through the open window,
primitive, simply melodic, without rhythmic sophistication,
unabashedly and unashamedly sensual. In the night that had
seemed to be going solid and weighted, it was a cry that said the
darkness had not died, that the body of the night had heart-life
still.

"That's a *batuque*," she said, singing the refrain. *"Quero*
chorar, não tenho lágrimas. I want to cry, but I have no tears."

"That's Brazil," he said. "More deeply Brazil than anything else I know."

"Yes," she said. "I'll miss it when I leave. I won't miss much else—not any longer. There was a time when I would have, but not now. How I hate the *gran finos* and their silly floating-flower lives, the false front of the Copacabana, like a stage setting imported from Europe. And how I hate myself for ever thinking I wanted it all." She paused and listened to the music once more. "But I want to remember that crying. I don't ever want to forget that."

"They laugh so much here," he said. "No wonder in their music they want to cry and don't have any tears."

The women's voices carried the words, soaring and quivering, seeming to fall back into the deep and resonant under-boom of the men. The sound was like a rocking arm beneath them both, cradling their weariness, and they sat back for a while without talking, wanting merely to listen.

"When Charles and I first arrived, I liked it better here than any place I had ever known," she said finally. "Somewhere in the back of the mind all of us dream of a country that is love's. Perhaps it is because in the fairy stories we read when we are children love makes everything beautiful. The witch is really only a princess in disguise, the Beast a Prince Charming. And, of course, where they live happily ever after is the most beautiful country on earth. We will always remember this country. It is the one place we can never forget. I suppose I thought I had found it once and for all when we came to Brazil. The mountains, the sea, the clear blue of the sky, were fabulous, the perfect background to what I was feeling. Finally, the landscape was not background but part of the feeling itself as though there were nothing antipathetic in the world and I could reach out and touch a rock, a flower, a tree, and know it to be love's. Now I don't feel that any more, and I can't really see Brazil at all. I suppose that is why I want to leave it. I don't like hospitality, and I want to see again."

She spoke now without pausing, without even waiting for

44

the conventional linking sentences that he might have inserted. It was not a monologue of self-absorption or indifference but of intense awareness of his presence, of an urgent sense of the need for fluency between them which she, being on the surface at least less constricted and diffident than he, must supply. Consequently, she talked steadily, intimately, and inclusively lest a silence occur, as in the car on the way to the apartment, and an intangible thickness coagulate and make communication slow to a laborious stop.

"When Charles told me four months ago that he wanted to go back to Paris, I knew he would not take me with him," she said. "He did not say so then, but I knew that he would expect me to understand in time, and that I would not go. He was French all the way through, very passionate, very complete in love, and very sure when it was over. My use was a thing of time, neatly measured so as not to last one day beyond boredom.

"To be the lover who does not lose, it takes precision in judging others, and the incapacity for regret, and Charles always saw things with a terrible precise clearness. He was afraid of growing old, and I had begun to remind him of the fact that he would. No man wants to live in a museum of what he was. He can go back there in memory but not live there. Charles saw the future clearly. It was my fault that I kept it vague and undefined."

He was glad that she was talking, since he himself was not ready to talk, being closer to memory, and he knew that she would come, as she had, to that point in the past where the rupture was, the point from which they must, if ever, proceed. He was thankful for the flow of her words. The ample talkativeness of women, he thought, is often a thing to be thankful for. In a moment of tension, it will do its best to push remembering forward into not-remembering or spread it horizontal and thin like water on a dry field to be sucked up and lost from sight. Silence is the cause of much of our suffering, the keeping of grief within us, acute, perpendicular, unreleased, and women, he felt, knew this better than men.

But, though he had not spoken, he knew that she was aware of the intensity of his response. It was she, ostensibly, who was moving them toward a starting point, but the tempo and extension of her conversation would not have been possible without his sympathy. Her words were the surface motion, but a hidden current, intuitive and deep, like a belt under a revolving tableau of figures and scenes, was moving them into conjunction.

When she paused at last for breath, they were once again, for a moment, silent, but the silence was not empty or formal but quivering with the reverberations of her words. She sat loosely against the sofa, her figure nowhere strict or taut, not fat but well-rounded, the body of a woman who, without fear of falling into excess, could stretch the sweetness of her senses a little beyond denial.

There are no rough edges in her, he thought. *She is gentle and hurt. Hurt and not able to hurt in return. The muscle of her heart is rich and strong but tired from loving, enduring, and not wanting to hurt. Now she is missing, needing the serenity of affection. Can I open in her the sealed-up power to touch again? Can I kiss her, touch her, taking the darkness of sensation into another darkness until there is warmth and the denial of darkness? To do this, to need to, to want to love again, to try in a passionate wanting.*

He moved very close to her, and put his arms around her. He did not look into her eyes because of his embarrassment and because he was ashamed of his desperation, of a desire to commit so soon a betrayal, of his wish to flood his loneliness with sensuous oblivion. Suddenly he was hearing, "Slowly, Robert. Not so fast. Wait a little." Said gently, tenderly resistive, at the same time that she rose and went into the other room.

Before they lay down, she lit a candle and placed it on the table beside the bed. At first, he was shy about the light, but then he was not, for it left them visible to each other and yet indistinct, hardly familiar at all, more like dream-figures, even strange to themselves, and perhaps this was better and easier for not remembering. The candle had been used before and was

46

encrusted with its own wax flesh and relic-weeping, and he thought that everywhere you looked in the world, at any hour, there was something broken, torn, crying, or frozen in an attitude where the crying had stopped. It was right that she had lit the candle, alive again now and liquid with fresh tear-form drippings, gleaming through all its cylindrical shape, dully so at the base, tipped with a tiny, molten, self-destroying crater where the flame, like an element antipathetic to the entombing wax, was almost disembodied from the wick. Without this light and its straining it would have been impossible, at first, to stay in the room. The night would have been too dense and they would not have been able to endure the muffling darkness without the wavering, shadow-shimmering flare of the candle whose almost incorporeal lucence moved, probing and pliantly caressive over the walls, bed, table, over them where they lay, as though to enter once more the thingness, the body, that it would, but finally, death-fearing, could not leave.

She did not undress entirely but lay there partially hidden from the candle glow like one who knew light and the absence of light, not calculating the risks, being incapable of doing so, but not rushing toward them either, knowing the pitiless price one pays for wanting to possess the beautiful whose possession always quivers with not-possession, bringing the final soulless wish not to have possessed at all.

As he looked at her, very quiet and waiting, with the light on her reddish hair, everywhere on the broad surface of her face except the recesses of her eyes which were dark and closed, he knew that he would always remember her saying, "Slowly, Robert. Not so fast. Wait a little." Not harshly spoken, but gently admonitive, as those who have suffered will admonish others who have also suffered but not so greatly as they.

Then she put out the light, and there was a moment of strange waiting and perilous equipoise in the darkness. And when he touched her, the touch of another was there. And when he kissed her, it was illusive and unreal since he could not kiss through memory, since he could not touch her really at all,

47

suddenly in the darkness remembering, not being able to forget, feeling that forgetting, in a lifetime, would hardly move fast enough or far enough to leave behind in silence one word of all that remembering.

And where his hand, his physical hand, reached—but without feeling—to accomplish the touch, he could imagine that she, too, would put her hand into another hand, and that their past lives were locked in a trance out of which they looked, as from emprisoned sleep, into the outrageous, shame-haunted, pent-eruptive world of dreams to see the fictive motions of their present lives.

It was then that he remembered—as memory will always make you remember a clear indestructible moment of the past just when the present struggles toward freedom—the departure and final passage of the boat seen from the window of his hotel, the boat, white, compact, poised like a bird on the water. The realization and shock-vision that within the boat was the other form, the other face, the absolute evidence of love. Within that boat moving, at first, slowly, almost laboriously and reluctantly, then quicker, more quickly, quicker, more quickly, quickly, quickly, quickly, until the sky at the far end of the harbor cracked open and, in a moment and forever, the boat drained out of consciousness.

Afterwards it was very quiet in the room. They lay there silently, unstirringly, as though in the darkness they were being watched hostilely from above. It was a long time before he dressed, and he began to wonder why she said nothing. But then he knew that her quietness was not anger, not silent reproach, not exclusiveness, not indifference, but deep patient waiting, the acceptance of not-possessing, the recognition of the vastness between one life and another.

At the door, she kissed him softly, without passion, and he wanted to cry out and shake his body for its obtuseness and his heart for its backward looking, but he did not. He could not. The sidewalk toward the city was steep and damp, and he had to walk down through the thick fog slowly, very slowly, to keep from falling.

48

A MORNING WAKE

WHY IN THE HELL DON'T THESE BIRDS COME, CRAN-
ford? I'm dying for a drink. I feel just like the Mojave inside.
Had quite a big night, you know — say, this samba is some
business. God, I ache like a whupped dog. How about you,
Girl?" The big man turned away from the Cultural Attaché,
who stood smiling at his elbow, and looked at his wife.

"Why I'm simply divine, darling. Like a jewel in a new setting. Wasn't that orchestra marvelous? And I must say I didn't
think you had it in you. I just feel like I've been crumpled in a
wonderfully wicked hand. It was better than my osteopath."

The tall, slender, young woman turned to Cranford as though
there had never been a man in the world she couldn't charm.
"You know what I mean, Mr. Cranford. The bones feel so delicious once you've been made aware of them. I suppose all of us
nowadays long to be broken over the wheel."

"Well, Mrs. Houston, after last night it probably wouldn't
hurt you. They say in Rio that the samba dissolves the skeleton,"
Cranford said. He was a sallow little man with a fixed yellow
grin.

"That's a good one, Cranford. Goddam it, that's just the way
I feel. Like some bastard bent me over backwards in a hoop and
rolled me down a rocky road—say, do you think it would do any
harm to go ahead and have a little drop? You know these fellows
better than I do." He shuddered. "God, I feel awful. My mouth
tastes like a Chinese family just moved out."

51

"I do think it would be better to wait. They're rather more formal down here than we are at home, you know." There was something of the undertaker in Cranford's solicitude. He tended his companion as though he were a potential body.

"Well, all right," Houston grumbled. "I don't want to get off on the wrong foot. But come on, let's take a load off our feet at least. That's quite a trip, you know. Miami, Rio, just like that. Gives you quite a bang." He moved slowly toward a corner of the long *salon* where the Brazilians were to be received. Dressed in a bright plaid tweed jacket and gabardine trousers, he looked extremely hot. His red hair and florid complexion seemed to heat up the air, fighting fire with fire, and his eyes glittered like indestructible little blue stones in the furnace of his flesh.

"Who's coming anyway? Some of the big boys, I hope. Let them know you're around, and the rest's a breeze. We want to do this thing right."

"Certainly, Mr. Houston. But since this is the first interview, I thought we'd start with a small group just to make it easy." Cranford hovered at Houston's back as though to catch him if he should fall. "Manoel Rodrigues is coming. He's one of the leading poets of Rio and, I might say, of all Brazil. João da Costa Marques, the regional novelist, since I thought you'd have a lot in common. Then, Vinicius de Oliveira, one of the best of the younger writers. Raul Liberal, another one of the older group of poets. And Octavio Morales, the critic of the *Correio da Manhã*. He'll be important to you."

"I suppose they know who I am and all that sort of thing."

"Oh, certainly, Mr. Houston." The wax smile stretched to its limits. "The Press Attaché did a grand job. I'll send you some clippings."

"You needn't bother. I've gotten so I don't read that sort of stuff any more."

"I understand. In this case, though, I don't think you'd make a mistake looking them over. There's been a lot of interest in your arrival, and you might want to know what they're thinking.

You see, you're the only American author of note who's ever been here. You'll be a sort of new species."

Houston blinked as though a barber had just held up the mirror and showed him the face of another man.

"Yeah? Well, maybe they'll want to put me in a cage, huh? Sometimes I wonder—"

Cranford made a rapid movement of his hand, brushing away some invisible annoyance in the air.

"I'd say the most important thing is your being here."

"Glad to hear you say that. I almost backed out at the last minute, you know. Nearly got bogged down in Washington. State kept hanging things on me till I felt like a Christmas tree for export. But Nan and I got a good shaking out in Miami, and I could see that the thing to do was just to come on down."

"Doodie always worries so." Mrs. Houston's voice groped confidingly toward the Cultural Attaché. "You have no idea, Mr. Cranford. The night before we left Miami, he just stood at the window for hours looking at nothing. I told him to stop trying to see Brazil before we got there."

"That's my Girl, Cranford. I don't know what I'd do without her. She's one of the 'don't run, walk' type. Pulls me through every time."

The three of them sat down on the dark green leather chairs and sofa, looking a little lonely on the brink of waiting for the others. Cranford lit cigarettes all around, feeling that he had gotten them over the little crisis very nicely. So far, so good. They hadn't started in drinking yet, and, at this rate, they would probably stay sober until the interview was over. If everything went smoothly, he could write a first-rate dispatch to the Department. Houston wasn't a Faulkner or a Hemingway, but he would do very well for the present. Even in Brazil, nearly everybody had heard about the Alabama author, his novels on sharecropper life, and his play, "Cotton Country," which had had such a long run on Broadway.

While Houston rumbled on lazily about the inconveniences of the morning, Cranford amused himself by recalling the little

53

conferência he had given about him at the Instituto Brasil—
Estados Unidos in preparation for his arrival. Yes, that had gone
very well too. He had been able to enliven his text considerably
by liberal quotations from *Authors in America,* and no one had
known the difference. There had been a good, serious, dignified
part where the critic spoke of Houston's early work as being
motivated by savage indignation. It had been easy enough too
to leave out the other side, what another critic in a derisive
moment had called his "decline into breast sellerdom," advising
Houston to "take off the false phallus before the public discovered his impudence." He had not needed to mention either
that Houston was the most popular American author in Soviet
Russia.

Cranford looked at his charge with a little tremor of amusement. Wilted and rumpled in his chair, the big, hulking man
was a somewhat damaged facsimile of the most recent photographs of himself in the magazines, posed, glass in hand, as a
Man of Distinction. Cranford wondered what dim, Messianic
urge had impelled him to take on an assignment from *Life* to
do a series of articles on Brazil and at the same time to accept a
tie-up with the State Department as a sort of unofficial cultural
ambassador.

The clerk at the desk of the Gloria had told Cranford all
about their arrival. A secretary was hired immediately, a special
writing desk hauled into their suite, and a long while spent
talking back and forth with the agent in New York as though
long distance calls might lace the two continents together, closing some wound in consciousness. The desk clerk had found the
author irritable and haphazard, but, with all, bluffly engaging,
and he had made allowances for temperament, promising Cranford to extend the full courtesy of the hotel.

"Don't you think it's about time they got here, Cranford?"
Houston suddenly asked, turning away from his wife, glaring
into the Attaché's face, calling him back on stage almost roughly. "I can't wait all day, you know."

54

Cranford gave one of his most demulcent smiles, and was just preparing to launch a conciliatory speech about the land of *Amanhã* when the guests arrived. As soon as they sat down, Houston hailed the waiter for drinks all around, a double Scotch for himself and Nan, vermouth for the Brazilians, a request relayed through Cranford who ordered an orange juice for himself.

"These gentlemen speak English, of course, Cranford. I'm afraid my Spanish is pretty rusty, high-school stuff, you know," Houston said, finding himself inclosed in a circle of expectant faces.

"Portuguese, you mean, Mr. Houston, naturally," Cranford said, smiling with seething embarrassment.

"Oh, sure, did I say Spanish?" The security of a drink in hand had begun to give him a brotherly glow, and he beamed around at them with rugged good humor. "Well, Cranford, I suppose we'd better get started. There'll be some questions, I imagine. I'd like to start off by saying I'm glad to be here. I came all the way down just to say hello. I think you've got a grand country, and I want you to know that all of us up there are good friends of yours." He pointed toward the North.

On at least two or three of the faces that looked at him there was a vacuous, pleasant lack of comprehension, and Cranford whispered hurriedly about the possibility of speaking French, but Houston drew back as if cuffed on the ear.

There was a heavy pause fraught with uncertainty as to how long the taut little scimitars of smiles could hang in all their faces. Mrs. Houston, who had a quick eye for slow motion grinding to a standstill, bubbled forth, "Oh, Doodie, what does it matter? We'll get along. These gentlemen don't mind. They know we're all so dumb at languages."

The little metallic grins cracked into laughter, dissolving the awkwardness of the verbal barrier like an international shyness.

"Let him speak English. I listen, I understand, I cannot speak," Rodrigues, the old poet said. He was a little fellow of

55

phthisical frailty with a charming pinched-up spout of a face which promised to give itself only drop by drop. He, as were his companions, was dressed in black.

"Oh, don't worry, Mr. Rodrigues," Mrs. Houston continued gaily. "Mr. Cranford can be our interpreter." And she motioned to the Attaché as though he should stand between them like a wall of glass. "Let's just talk back and forth as we please." She smiled freely and made cordial gestures all around, speaking, as it were, with her body. She looked extremely beautiful in her modish white dress with touches of astringent gold in her jewelry.

"Sure, sure," Houston chimed in though he had begun to sweat, a stigmatic ray of the sun across his face. "Let's just talk. That's what I'm here for. Ask me a few, then I'll ask a few—you can ask me anything," he finished blindly, looking around at the faces which had a murky green-white cast to them, strangely so he thought for a people one thought of as living in the open air. They seemed to absorb his ebullience, waiting for a chance to say a darker thing to him. Somehow they were almost legendary, shadowy and inaccessible figures of a fable he had been a long time trying to tell. It was a foolish notion, he knew, but they brought with them that feeling of the verge which sometimes came over him at home when his usual pleasures had lost their "zing" and his other refuge had temporarily failed him, his power to summon men, women, actions, and ideas from his imagination like a supporting cast around his life. They almost seemed to him to represent a residual world of which his words for so long a time had been an enemy.

"What do you think of Hemingway, Mr. Houston?" Vinicius de Oliveira, the young writer, spoke English without difficulty. He was lighter in color than the others, with eyes of startling blue like fresh-pressed flowers. He was known around town for his *avant garde* Americanism.

"Oh, him," Houston said blankly. "Good man, good man. I make it a practice of never talking about colleagues." Then turning away from his audience of one he spoke into Cranford like a megaphone he had just picked up. "Tell them I don't claim to be an artist, Cranford. I'm just a hard worker and believer like them. Nothing fancy about me. I like people and believe in words." He spoke vigorously now, like a man defending himself from the charge of being effeminate.

"You mean that literature is a concussion between the two?" Cranford asked, vastly pleased.

For a moment Houston looked at him as if a dictaphone had talked back. "Yes, tell them that. That sounds good."

The little band of Brazilians kept looking at the American, expectation not yet quite dimmed from their eyes. Houston's bold, bright look had a ruddy sun-like quality, and they with their dark clothes and pale faces seemed willing to be shadows of the light, tatters of the parent orb. There was a kind of longing in the way they waited for him to speak, an attitude of respect which some idea of him had earned long before his arrival. But he shifted in his chair uneasily and said nothing for a long moment, leaving Cranford with his mouth open, dry as an exhausted river bed, waiting for the fluency of sound.

He finally looked up like an old savage king who had called a parley only from long-time habit. "Tell them I'm here to write a series of articles about their great country. And I need their help. Tell them that, Cranford. We need each other. I suppose that's the main thing an American has to say. I want to get around down here, meet everybody and see everything."

During the time-lag of translation, Houston watched the faces of the Brazilians as though already he had thought of something else and would like to rush through the tube of Cranford's voice and call back his sentences. There had been nothing wrong with what he had said. They were the same simple words he had used hundreds of times before. They were democratically "safe"—they had the tone of the common man carefully blended in them, they were protocol for any American abroad. Twenty years ago when he had taken as a sort of epigraph for his life Whitman's "Not till the sun excludes you do I exclude you," they would have sounded just right. Now they were unattached

57

to any feeling he could identify as his own. God, I must be getting old, he thought. The old echo chamber doesn't work any more.

All the while Mrs. Houston kept chattering along in English and Houston saw with pleasure that she was superbly effective, like a fountain of instinct which nothing stanched. Though she made no effort at all, the eyes of the Brazilians wandered restfully toward her. She had the transparent kind of loveliness which if you looked long enough didn't seem to be there at all, but there was her voice, apart from any language denotation, which played in the air its iridescent stream. She moved among them as in an area of drouth, making stunted little sentences in English flower from their mouths, and they nodded, smiled, and passed their good feelings on from one to another.

"The Girl's all right, isn't she?" Houston said on the side to Cranford. "She's better at this stuff than we are. You should see how she handles the press at home. Great girl—let's have another round, Cranford. We're all getting a little dry."

While they were waiting for the drinks, the Brazilians talked guiltily among themselves, trading subjects for translation. Liberal, an enormous balloon of a man, so fat that he might have contained a pump that released gaseous matter within him, looked turgid with frustration, letting out excited little puffs of words to his friends. Morales, who was a spastic, kept opening and closing his mouth laboriously like a rusty vise, but nothing came out. Cranford, hearing them agree to engage Houston on the subject of contemporary French literature, fluttered the gills of his eyes helplessly while the translation passed through him like poisoned water.

Houston listened with a faraway look as though France too were a place he would one day go and leave something of himself, but he shook his head dreamily, letting the subject drift away to Mrs. Houston who caught it like a Carnival balloon where she sat under a bright little tent of talk with Oliveira. There was now an indefinable draft blowing back and forth through the voice of Cranford. It promised in time to be as

58

clammy and chilly as the exhalation of a cave. Finally Houston roused himself and dropped the conversation like a ponderous burden he had been lugging through a tunnel.

"Ask these gentlemen if any of them like to fish, Cranford. I'd like to do a little while I'm here. Clears the brains. We might go out together, one at a time. It would give us a chance to get better acquainted and talk over some of these matters. I might learn a little Portuguese by then. Anyhow it's easier to talk when you're not trying—you know what I mean? Nan knows that. Just look at her go. She ought to be an Ambassador. Maybe she's the best we've got to offer." He smiled heartily and immediately caught everyone's attention, the little ring glowing together, contracting like a crown. But then the idea of fishing returned, and the Brazilians looked mournfully capsized.

Houston began to feel irritably lonely, and, once again, he didn't know exactly why he had come. It had seemed a wonderful thing to do at the time, for he had lately begun to think of himself as a man who was at home everywhere and could make others feel so. He had been willing to come and be among them, and it was that idea that had always been at the bottom of his work—whatever bitterness was there had been for those who were against this idea.

If he had been brave enough—yes, perhaps it came down to that—he might have pushed on and told them a fishing story anyway. He knew some good ones and had already done a few for the magazines after his Southern stuff had begun to run out. They made him feel better now than the earlier work, and he would have liked to see how they struck a foreign ear. But he had started wrong—he had made the fatal error of the storyteller, something he could never have done when he sat at his desk—he had made them believe that the story belonged to himself alone, that it had a personal thesis, that a man was going to tell it only for men like himself. He had forgotten to free the story for their own affectionate interests. Somehow they had sensed that if they let him go on, he would soon be hitting

59

them over the head with *his* idea of fishing. He had forgotten to use the proper tone, "Once upon a time—," the easy, relaxed, unobtrusively inclusive true teller's way so that the voice in the story was more than the voice of one man, and each passed along the human voice, maintaining the dialogue of life, "keeping up the conversation" among men.

But it was too late now, for the meeting had taken on a funereal atmosphere, and the talk was of those who had come together out of respect for a deceased, distant relative. They all took turns looking vacantly down at the floor as though within their circle lay the corpse which might inspire them to a common feeling.

Through the open French doors the tropic morning seemed oppressively fecund and without allure. The intense blue water, the dazzling sunlight, the great mountains that seemed to bulge within themselves suggested a natural syncrasy of power driving the individual back upon himself. It seemed to hit Houston in the face like a flaming brand, and he wondered why he had not fallen back before, stopped and realized where he was.

He remembered that the earth had looked him in the face like this years ago when he was a lanky, red-headed boy on his father's dusty Alabama farm and that he had determined to talk back to it, to find something specifically human to say. And he had done so, he had spoken out and spoken out through the years until one day the Voice seemed monumental, immobile, and imprisoned within him, and he had lost the dexterity of giving it motion and projection, while all around him the world continued to grow, fructify, and proliferate beyond all range of words.

The whisky had begun to really work at last, giving him the old tumid feeling of existence which, though better than a headache, was these days itself not altogether pleasant; sometimes, as now, almost like a flood-back of pressure from a vast, gaudy balloon he had been blowing all his life. What had been projected and expanded and diffused swelled back for its own kind of retaliation. It gave him a heavy, perilously dilating—

60

what he would have called a "global"—feeling, and the thin, tight skin covering his awareness longed for some old, strong, hairy pelt such as the cave man wore when he sat around the fire and began to tell his first stories of the night beyond.

Mrs. Houston (bless the Girl, thought Houston, so Goddam quick to haul me out) suggested "rotating chairs" whereby each one of the guests had a chance to sit briefly beside him. This was an old trick they had used so successfully at home where it seemed to give them all a glow. But now, Rodrigues coming first, then Liberal, Marques, Oliveira, and finally Morales, it was like a condoling of the bereaved, and each was glad when the circular contact started again. Morales was most difficult. His eyes bulged with a plethora of communication, the words not able to reach their natural outlet, and his mouth hung open, gaping, while all the little groups grew still as though waiting for a birth.

"This is a quick trip," Houston finally said, digging deep down in his reserves of poise, summoning a climactic air. "I'm coming back again and stay with you a long time and really get to know you. And you must come up our way—We've got to do something about this, this—" And he looked off and away, where what was mirrored against time had no name.

Each of the Brazilians managed a quick, graceful compliment, an allusion to one of his books, and then it was time to go. Their hands were cold and damp, but Houston felt his own gloved in fire as though he had picked up the wrong end of a welding iron.

"This has been delightful, gentlemen. Simply delightful," Mrs. Houston said, rising graciously, lifting the svelte jet of her manner among them for the last time. "You must send us your books. We'll read them somehow. Mr. Cranford will help us, I'm sure." The Brazilians shook her hand with the look of men who thought that much would be forgiven her.

Houston took them to the elevator, his hang-over throbbing in him once again, and he felt dizzy as if the planet had stumbled beneath him. The green, white, dark blur of the Brazilians

61

was like the color of a vertigo, but, as he continued to look with all his might, they were gone, sucked down by the elevator, like an ancient, bilious-tinted headdress some unamenable idea had finally tossed into the cavern of the hotel. The air was free again; it broke dazzlingly through the window with all its age-old brilliance once more unsullied. For a moment it made the *salon* like a house of mirrors, blinding all vision, obscuring even the reflection of himself, stabbing in behind his eyes until his brain ached as from a surgical knife.

He turned back and walked toward Mrs. Houston and Cranford, a great figure of rust and gold, wondering why there were so few railings in the world a man could lean upon.

"Well, Girl, I need a drink. How about a short one before lunch?"

Now that he had nothing more to translate, Cranford stood there looking at them reproachfully like a man of *papier-mâché* who might have to wait a very long time for the Voice to fill him with its visceral timbre.

A CHARIOT OF FIRE

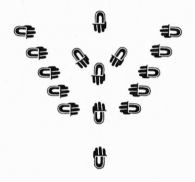

"OH, MY DEAR, THIS IS A HOLY TRIP, A PILGRIMAGE. It'll be the one thing you'll most remember about Brazil." Trompowsky looked at the American girl with a misty, dreamy expression in his eyes. "I've made it many times, once every few years. Back to the source, I call it. A day in Ouro Preto and my heart beats red again." He laid a pale, slender hand across his chest.

The girl from Sedalia, Missouri, stirred a little in her seat and smiled to show a polite interest. Two hours ago she had told him that was where she was from, that her name was Ella MacDonald, and that she was an art student now living in Rio. Nothing more, but he was a man of a deep reservoir of conversation, thoroughly at ease in English, ready to release a water-flow of words across any aridity of silence that surrounded him. Now the story of his life was spread out around them in a great expanse, from the day of his decision to leave Russia and make a life for himself in Brazil, through his "storm and stress," to the venerable years of success and popularity. Ella floated in the warm bath of his personality, overcome as well by the torpor of her own timidity. But she was used to being the ballast of another's ego. Long ago her mother, in a fit of anger, had told her that she was heavy, lethargic. Maybe the old gentleman was like the others. Perhaps he was trying to buoy her up, awaken her to life through the sense of his own, "get a rise out of her," as they said back home.

65

He needn't have talked to her so long, she reflected. Such a monologue must have taxed his ingenuity and been exhausting even for one of his capacious self-interest. Perhaps he had taken pity on her, thinking her lonely—she nearly always managed to look that way. But that was better than aversion, which was the other side of her brief gamut of response from human beings. Yes, she told herself, he had understood everything when he took a look at her: the stringy yellow hair, the prominent spectacles like showcases of her harrowed introspection, the face bruised with an expression of self-hatred, the figure rather too angular for a woman, the plain, blowzy clothes like a final flaunting of the soul's despair. All of which had enabled him to enjoy his benignity from the moment when he sat down beside her this morning. He looked bland, replete, she thought, rather like a plump bluebird gone gray, a blue tam rakishly set upon his head in a remnant tuft of color and his eyes like blue blemishes on the residual pallor of his skin. *Plump and stuffed with worms*—the thought appealed to the macabre in her.

"Are we nearly there?" she asked, feeling taut, and yet very much alive beside his comfortable casualness.

"Yes, one more hump of the hills and we'll be at the train stop where we can take the car. But *paciência,* as our good Brazilians say, you're moving away from time not into it. It won't matter there." He waved a hand into the future. "Time's all bottled up back in Rio. Here we drink eternity."

"Can't they sometimes be the same?" she asked, once again hating him for his fluency. "Isn't the eternal merely the quality of passion we bring to time?" It was a peculiar spurt of eloquence for her, more like an eruption than a statement, and she felt like a "gaga" art student afterwards.

"How well you speak!" he said, smiling mockingly. "Here I've been running on, and yet you have so much to say. Tell me about your life in Rio. Are you happy there, my dear? Tell me what you do with your spare time." He gave a little yellow grin, almost snickering, and she shuddered inwardly at the fulsome way he tended her.

66

"I paint. That's all. I just paint every day. I study at the Escola de Belas Artes. This is my holiday, the first in three years. I've come to see the Aleijadinho in Ouro Preto." She felt rock-like again and regretted more than ever her sudden jet of speech. Now she knew she would not go through her biography with him and give him another chance for pity. If he asked her about her life again, she would say, "It's been tough," looking at him arrogantly; and suddenly, instead of awkward and timid, he would think her rough, mannish, and would squirm a little inside, which would be all to the good.

"Oh," he said, having absorbed her interruption commodiously, "you must let me show you around Ouro Preto. What a treat to show it to an artist—you know so few of them come here from Rio."

"Maybe they're better off there. Maybe they've got sense enough to know that even if they came they'd stay at home."

"Not at all. Not at all." He looked at her a little archly, but even his pique, she decided, was pert rather than incisive. "They'd profit by taking a look at the past. They're mad all of them. Their work's a mish-mash. As for me, I come to Ouro Preto to talk with the past, to learn its great old secrets. Then I go home and paint my canvases—and look how the public buys them. They're thirsty for a drink of the past, the fine old wine instead of the absinthe of modernism which others give them. We're all infected, but a few of us have enough sense to take the cure. Ah, my dear, Ouro Preto is my sanatorium. Always I leave a part of my soul here for convalescence, and when the other sickens in Rio, I return and take my health again."

So this is a corpse I sit beside, by its own admission, a corpse, Ella thought with grisly humor, and the figure of the old man, loaded with his death, trundling back and forth between the present and the past as though his soul were workng in two shifts, seemed ridiculous, comic, and—if she let herself go—pathetic. That she should have met him this morning just a few hours before the end of the journey gave her a feeling of having suffered a relapse, as though her thoughts had produced

67

him in a kind of lost, backward-looking delusion, anticipating some exquisitely self-torturing contrast to be made with whatever lay ahead—whatever it was that kept pulling her toward it magnetically as though her body were made of a kindred but resistant substance. All night long when she sat up, alone, she had this feeling of vital attraction radiating through the heavy, lumbering train which sometimes seemed restrained and wound in the vine of the mountain or like a prong squeezing through a gap in the darkness. Then the caul of night burst into the peculiarly deflated mood of morning, and this spectral little creature had sat down beside her, proved himself all too abundant and bodily, and left her at last glad of his presence as a foil of the unknown and angry that his volubility had robbed her of her "approach" to the old town. She felt dizzy now, as though from train sickness, and would have liked to touch him and even lean against him, but the very thought of his corpulence made her shiver for what was strong and firm—a stalwart, angular, bony man, for only that could have stopped the swaying in her mind.

Still they must ride to the hotel together for taxis were scarce and expensive, but she resolved to shake him there. On the way, as Trompowsky sat smugly and silently beside her, once again she had a feeling of Rio, of having brought part of the city with her out of some perverse connivance of the soul, and the taxi, weighted in a mechanical somnolence, moved slowly, like a hearse through this quiet and sleeping town which might have been a tomb, a dream in glass, or a citadel without besiegement in a fantasy of the mind. But the conflict of its identity revolved in Ella's thoughts as though her own clear preconceived idea of it did a dervish, blending these facts of reality glimpsed from the car with Trompowsky's presence, the world from which she had traveled, into a vertigo whose peril as motion seemed equaled only by the threat of its peril as pause. At the center of the little whirlpool that was she, a voice, like a failing echo of her own, said: *This is not it, this is not as it should be, this is not as it was planned.* She pressed her foot hard upon the floorboard, clamping the body in its place, as though, despite the fall, the swoon, which might follow, that rotation must be stopped. The pretext of the lurching car allowed her to take Trompowsky's arm, and, though certain that it would be too unsubstantial to sustain her grasp, she clutched through the flabby flesh to the bone, and felt it hold.

"You'll find the hotel very comfortable, my dear," he said, as they rolled up to the entrance. "It was built by the Government five years ago. Good mattresses on the beds. A nice, clean place."

A minute ago he was spouting off about the past, she thought. *But when he goes to bed at night he wants to lie down in the Twentieth Century, sleep its sleep, and wake and look through the window—and voilà—the past, the beautiful past!*

The hotel jutted on the side of the hill, white and gleaming, faced with glass like a sterilizing box. She knew it would be brilliantly sunlit, warm, and a little steamy inside, languorous, but unassailably comfortable. It struck her as really more obsolete than anything in town, obtrusive among the unity of age, so that you wanted to reverse the perspective of the years and see it as a kind of cave-dwelling there on a ledge of rock.

"I didn't expect this," she said to Trompowsky.

"No one does," he answered with a silly little grin. "But it's here for use, my dear. There was so much complaint from tourists that the Ministry of Education had to do something about it. But you needn't let it interfere. When you go outside, the whole town's a cathedral.—Shall we meet for lunch? We might go to the Igreja de São Francisco afterwards. There's some of the best Aleijadinho there."

"Oh, thanks, thanks an awful lot." Caught so suddenly with his offer, she was more cordial than she meant to be. "I'm feeling a little shaken up after the trip. I think I'll have a sandwich in my room and rest awhile. I may look around town a little this afternoon, and save the sculptures for tomorrow."

69

"Just as you like." Trompowsky turned around and busied himself officiously at the desk. He did not bother to sign for them both, but handed her the pen and moved quickly down the corridor, rotund and buoyant, like a grayish balloon with a blue patch on its top.

When she had finished signing the register, the clerk looked at her card in the most professional manner and asked, "How long will we have the pleasure of your company, Miss Mac-Donald?" He spoke book-English, all the words correctly pronounced, but sounding like something memorized.

"Oh, several days, I suppose. It depends. You seem to have plenty of room." She spoke curtly, glancing around the empty lobby.

"Oh, yes, yes. It's merely for the Ministry's records. We hope you'll stay as long as possible. You are our guest, Miss MacDonald. We are honored."

"Oh," she said, and looked rather crossly at him, wondering why the Brazilian petty official always had to dress in black and display the manners of an undertaker. She was prepared not to like him, although she knew he was what Libby, her roommate back in Rio, would call a "cute boy." At the same time, she would have liked to say something to him, attracting him favorably, something that would make heat waver in his eyes and make him forget to call her "Miss." But he was like all the rest, sensing her hostility as an animal does, but all the worse for being so polite, so unctuously solicitous. She would have liked to slap him and stamp a look of anger in the smooth dough of his face. This streak of violence made her feel crude, ashamed of herself, and yet she longed for just that—to slug it out with someone and get an honest response, a slap in return, an oath, and afterward, perhaps, an impassioned truce, some basis for true friendship. But it hadn't worked with men or women, especially the young—she had known a few older men who were willing to exchange confidences, but they were too gentle and complacent, and she ended by despising them as impotent and

70

weak. It was Whitman's *Camerado* she longed for, someone ardent in friendship. She had tried the direct approach, the blunt appeal for sincerity, even on Libby who had told her to go and "work out on a punching bag."

Her room was exactly what she expected: a square, sunlit cubicle of the Twentieth Century. After eating a crumpled sandwich from her bag, she threw herself across the low bed for a half hour's nap, partly to avoid Trompowsky, partly to make herself fresh for what she had traveled so far to see.

When she woke, it was dark, and there was a soft, misty rain falling. She could not imagine how she had slept so long, a deep, unfigured, dreamless sleep which was unusual for her. But the rest had not made her feel altogether free and unburdened—maybe her dreams were lying in wait for her—and she thought of the coming night with a little anticipatory thrill of terror. After eating the last sandwich in her bag and drinking part of a bottle of mineral water brought along for the train trip, she put on her trench coat and slipped quietly by the clerk at the desk, aware that he whisked his head around when she passed through the door as though a phantom had glided past.

The rain had stopped, but the whole town was enveloped in a womb of mist. It had been good to slip out of the hotel surreptitiously like a fading back into time. She walked down the moist cobblestones of the street carefully, admiring the old baroque buildings with their scrolls and contorted curves, their gilded woods and plasters, now partly rusted away. The richness and elaboration—the adorning hand was everywhere present—made her think with a shudder of her little modern cell in the hotel, constructed as though personal life, too, could be run like a machine. But now on all sides was the mark of humanity, nothing impersonal and merely functional. The mood of the town was very compact, she decided, one of age leaning upon age, and thereby ready to endure the pressures of time, knowing it held its story of youth and struggle intact behind a shield of persistence. *So this is the city of gold,* she whispered to herself, *Ouro*

71

Preto, Black Gold, the gold in the earth, the flesh of the slave. And the white hands twining, twining . . . the light and the dark braided together in an old chain of endeavor and suffering.

Up the steep hill the figure of a man enveloped in a long black raincape and wearing a broad black hat glided toward her with apparitional ease. Under the lamplight, his face was lean and sharp with an El Greco elongation in the bone structure.

"Boa noite, Senhora," he said as he went by, and Ella had the feeling that if she stopped him, his greeting would have been repeated in echoes of two hundred years ago. He was like a fume, a somber exhalation of the past. She thought suddenly of Aleijadinho who was the real reason for her journey—the passer-by had aroused a specter of the crippled artist who undoubtedly had ascended this street on his way to work. The mist melted away around his memory, and she could see him on a day of clear poised weather, of balanced light and equilibrium in the world, helplessly borne by slaves, himself the son of a slave and a Portuguese master carpenter, the disfigurement of his face veiled and his body hidden in a flowing cape—the leper who had done his last work with chisel and mallet strapped to the stumps of his fingers. His flesh had become the burden of chaos which the maker must bear, his illness and suffering were the smothering corset he wore, and all that the soul could do was the impossible, break out, break through, ascend: release the shining figure. Twist, turn the eyes of the lazar inward until they yielded the angel face. Twist, turn, until the stone revolved within itself and showed the countenance of the soul. The gyration of the true man outward, the torsion of the flesh until it freed the captive. No wonder the hand, tutored in ecstasy, could touch the stone with light until it mirrored the struggling and revolving vision turning to a calm. Ella thought grandly of how long that revolution in the soul must have taken, the artisan making himself artist, alone, without teachers, repeating in arduous conquest the whole history of man as maker, pent in the lonely hinterland of the world, caught in the prison of misshapen flesh. Somewhere in the Brazilian earth nearby the resinous

72

torch of that body lay quenched, but tomorrow, and Ella glowed with the thought, she would see the captured and arrested light in the work of its hands.

When she returned to the hotel, Trompowsky was waiting in the lobby, his face startlingly pallid in contrast to the dark brilliance of her reverie.

"I've been missing you, my dear. Come and have a Guaraná or a coffee with me," he said.

"Thank you, no. I'm rather done in from my walk. I think I'd better go to bed early." She was determined not to be caught this time. It occurred to her that she might twit him about the Guaraná—a nasty mixture of ground seed, sugar, and a shot of rum if so desired—an old Indian drink supposed to stimulate virility.

"Come sit a bit," he insisted, grinning, wetting his pale lips with his tongue. "I want to talk to you about a proposition you should be interested in. I've been thinking you'd make a good secretary. You're intelligent, you're an artist, and you know Portuguese very well. The one I've got now is such a fool, mad about the young men. You should think it over. I'm very good to my girls."

He looked at her steadily, and—was it her imagination?—a leer flickered over his face, quickly undulant, covered by the returning wave of his paternal air.

"Oh, I don't think I would do," she said hastily. "I've had no experience. Besides, I'm down here on a scholarship. I couldn't walk out on that. There's my work, you know."

"Certainly, certainly, there would be plenty of time for that. I'll go over your drawings with you every day."

"But—" She looked at him, her face reddening, befuddled with anger.

"There's no hurry, there's no hurry," he said interrupting. "Think it over. We can talk about it tomorrow." He drained his glass and rose to leave. "You know, my dear, I could be like a parent to you."

Ella felt like crying when she reached her room. But once in

73

bed, she flooded her mind with a pleasant fantasy of the past recalling her father, and soon she could hear the sound of his voice, gentle and manly. There in his old great chair he sat and she sat at his feet on a stool while he read from a worn Bible. His eyes were dark and penetrating, luminous with spiritual force, and they would have seemed terrible had they not been kind. But his body was slender and frail, burdened with its restless sensibility like a delicate candle with an enormous aura of flame. He was reading one of their favorite passages, the story of Elijah and then of Elisha and the Shunamite's son, letting his voice quiver with feeling: *And when Elisha was come into the house, behold, the child was dead, and laid upon his bed. He went in therefore, and shut the door upon them twain, and prayed unto the Lord. And he went up, and lay upon the child, and put his mouth upon his mouth, and his eyes upon his eyes, and his hands upon his hands: and he stretched himself upon the child; and the flesh of the child waxed warm. Then he returned and walked in the house to and fro; and went up, and stretched himself upon him: and the child sneezed seven times, and the child opened his eyes. And he called Gehazi, and said, Call this Shunamite. So he called her. And when she was come in unto him, he said, Take up thy son.* Ella felt this resuscitation tremble through her body, and she was terrified when her mother entered the room where she and her father sat together in perfect sympathy.

At first, her mother's mouth was long and hard like the barrel of a gun, and her first words would be a shower of bullets. Then her presence grew and spread, metallic and heavy, like an enormous candle-snuffer above the flame of her father's beautiful voice. Just as they were about to be enclosed in the descending mold of darkness, Ella screamed into wakefulness, and lay shivering in her bed. The solidity of her loneliness settled about her, and she thought of the old village outside that she loved but which held no friend for her except a dead man, and she thought of Trompowsky, somewhere nearby, the soft jelly of his body swathed in an elegant night suit, stretched out in complete compliance with the night, snoring flabbily, and she knew that if she should have to escape it would be toward him alone that she could run, and the world seemed ominous with his accidental power.

The morning was clear and flawless, and Ella woke "in focus," as she told herself, feeling the day to be a gift. Trompowsky would not be up till nine or ten, she was sure of that, so she dressed rapidly, rushed downstairs for a glass of orange juice, a cup of coffee, and toast, and walked out into the lucid globe of the sunlight. *I shall set a form upon this day,* she said to herself, recognizing how much this habit of communion was growing on her in such a silent world. *It has been given to me to remember. I shall carry it away like a bubble of clear gold. Twenty years from now, yes, twenty years from now, I shall be able to stand in its center and remember as though it were the depth of my own heart I stood in.* She thrilled to the extravagance of her emotion, but was glad that no one in the world could hear what she was feeling.

Across the hills the dual towers of the churches rose, white and trimmed in a rich brown stone the color of weathered gold blending with the plastered walls in a tarnished chryselephantine effect. There, in the pathway toward these towers, was a radius of her morning, Ella thought, and, everywhere she looked, another and another. She let the natural magnetism of the highest church lead her to it, beautiful and imposing in itself seen from a distance, but melting away, almost dissolving into nothing as she approached and looked at the delicate sculptured scrolls of soapstone ascending in a buoyant whirl of cherubs thrown like a radiant wreath across the doorway. Inside there was the baptismal font, once again with convoluted stone and spiraling cherubs seeming to draw the essence of matter upward with it, the wall of the church itself bodiless and unsubstantial. And so, from church to church, Ella saw them in themselves, dominant on the hills, and felt them fading away and falling back from the radiation of the sculptures, until the ground was set and the air hung with emblems of a vision, so compact in adoration that the very marrow of the buildings had been drawn into them. She could not remember another world so decked with garlands and trophies of its passion. It seemed to her that at the Igreja de São Francisco de Assis she found the pivot of it all. Directly above the door a huge circular medallion had been set, showing St. Francis, kneeling, looking upward to his Brother, the Sun, whose rays contained him in a lambent nest. She thought of the dark, crippled, leprous man there on the scaffold working at this kneeling figure of rapt love as though each stroke could transfer his soul into the enduring stone.

All day Ella felt herself moving in shafts of sunlight. The night before with its dreams of her father, the beautiful flowing of his voice through the Biblical story that had always been a kind of pact between them, had left her keyed up and almost hectically receptive. Trompowsky in his little tam shuttled back and forth across the stream of the day like a blue, recurrent mote, seen once against the hill and again looking down at her in the square just after she had left one of the churches. He waved gaily and beckoned to her, but she pointed in a misleading direction, and let the day glide beneath her once more. She did not return to the hotel until nearly sundown, throwing herself across her bed for a short nap, the impact of the day charged through every fibre of her being. Once again she slept flawlessly, dreamlessly, waking in a stupor of darkness and the incredible knowledge that it had begun to rain mistily again. She felt terribly disappointed, having planned to see some of the churches at night, particularly Saint Francis, wanting to see it drenched with moonlight. There was nothing to do, she reflected as she rang the *portaria,* but have a quick bite in her room and take a look around anyway.

When the sandwich and tea were finished, she hurried downstairs and through the lobby, but the clerk stopped her.

"Oh, Miss MacDonald, Mr. Trompowsky has been asking for

you. He said to tell you he'd inquired." The clerk smiled—whether meaninglessly, or sententiously, she was not quite sure.

"Well, I'm sorry," she said, "but I've been terribly busy. Tell him I won't be able to see him this evening."

"Very well, Miss. He left this in your box."

"Thank you." She hurried on, looking at the little booklet, *A Guide To The Appreciation of Aleijadinho,* in Portuguese. The insolent old snob!

Once outside, Ella felt it could have been the night before. The same shrouding mist, the same silence, the figures in their raincapes passing at long intervals in a phantom chain. Her reverie as vague and clouded as the night, she did not know how long she had been walking when she saw, there at the far end of the lamplit arc, another black-swathed form come toward her, smaller than the rest, walking laboriously, seeming to hobble in the swirls of the voluminous cloak. She stopped, statically defined, while her heart dilated and was the only organ of her being. The figure came on toward her, dragging through the mist like a crippled ghost.

"Aha, Miss Ella. I've found you at last. You've been avoiding me." Under the rimmed hat Trompowsky's eyes were the blue-black of smooth sapphires. The light focused on his damp mouth which spilled out words like an old yellow spout.

"Oh, no, not at all. I had so much to see today. There simply wasn't time for anything else."

He came closer, and, as he leaned back in the light, she saw his whole face, so soft, so white, even the eyes drained pale, almost like a Halloween travesty of a ghost.

"I missed you," he said. "I kept sensing you everywhere—when I arrived, you'd just been there. It was like a chase. Quite the most exciting thing I've ever done here."

"Well, you've caught me at last. Here I am." She wanted to sound laconic, but knew, in desperation, that she probably sounded shy, confused.

"Yes, here we are. My dear, I don't know when I've been so struck with anyone. Such energy and such enthusiasm! So much you saw today! Really, it was quite a pursuit, I can tell you. And now I must hear all about it. Didn't I tell you it would be a holy trip? Didn't I say you would never get over it?"

On the way up the hill back to the hotel Trompowsky kept close, confidential, possessive, and she thought he would never stop telling her what she had seen, thought, and felt. He did not touch her, but she had the feeling that if he had, his hand would have struck her like a claw. The luminous box of the hotel seemed up an interminable hill of glass, and, though she wanted to push on alone, it was Trompowsky who had the spurs on his feet. When she sank immediately onto the sofa in the lobby, even he acknowledged her exhaustion and bid her goodnight.

The bed itself was like a box for Ella when she lay down, the final container within a container. She felt cold, heavy, spent, with little vibrations of heat flickering through her body in a mockery of life. If there had not been the fantasy world, like a fourth dimension of the mind, ample, unconfined, the empire of her safety, she did not know what she would have done. But there was her father speaking gently, soothingly, soothingly . . . then Elijah, the father, impassioned and powerful . . . Elisha, the son, asking that a double portion of the spirit descend upon him . . . Elisha walking across the room wearing a long cloak like a shield around his incandescence, a dust of stone flaking down from its folds. . . . He put his mouth upon her mouth, and his eyes upon her eyes, and his hands upon her hands, and she felt warmer than she had felt in all her life. When she reached up to him in embrace, the broad black hat fell backward in the light of adoration and Trompowsky's head slumped forward within the noose of her surrounding arms. Ella switched on the lights, reached for her glasses, and waited until dawn for the swaying of her body to be still.

No one saw her leave the next morning except the clerk who, stiff, tall, dark, stood like an exclamation point at the silent frenzy of her departure. At her bidding the taxi drove fast though the red mountain road was still wet from the rain. The

78

train stood on the tracks, black, ponderous, inexorably pointed toward Rio, and Ella knew it would contain her in a moment like a cylinder of her chosen fate, carrying her back to what old, what new, contention of desire. On the platform of the passenger car, she turned to see the taxi disappear at the rise of a hill, brilliantly streaked, splashed with color of flame, gone in a whirlwind of motion, and, as though a phantasmagoria of her journey were blent in that image, she whispered, "My father, my father, the chariot of Israel, and the horsemen thereof."

THE WHITE QUEEN

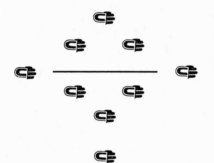

I WAS NEW AT THE GLORIA. THE FIRST SECRETARY in charge of housing the officers told me it was the only good hotel near the Embassy and that I had better stay there in the interests of my work. I took his advice since I was anxious to do the right thing, but I soon found out that most of the young, unmarried men lived at the swankier Copacabana, a long, languid drive from the Embassy, and I wondered if he had sensed in me a difference as though, perhaps, I should be closer to the center of indoctrination.

In any case, it was a happy choice for me. Apart from the comfort and beauty of the Hotel—it was done in the grand manner with capacious salons and rooms throughout, giving the sense of old fertilities still potent in its structure, nowhere suggestive of the white sterility of so many modern interiors—it suited my temperament. There had been a longing in me to live in the European way and, apparently, now I was to have the chance even though it were once removed from the ancient source. Nothing in my background, which had been totally American, could account for this longing. It was simply there, as though some stray seed from the Old World had drifted among the flesh of my people. Perhaps it was this desire to return to what I did not really know, a sort of wanderlust full of nostalgia but vague in the images of experience, that had been a motive in my entering the Foreign Service. I suppose I thought it would offer me various ways to attach my allegiance and embodiments of certain things which I wanted to believe important.

I was a little surprised at the deference with which I was treated at the Gloria. Used to the brisk, brusque treatment I had often had in the hotels at home, increasing an inherent feeling of insubstantiality, of not having been seen, I was delighted to indulge in the impression of "being somebody." I told myself that it was because I was good-looking, that I looked the part of the young, affluent, American careerist (for, you see, that part of me had always been certain—I had evidently been born with mirrors around me like a portable setting, and these pleasing reflections were the only solid conception I had) . In any event, every attention was paid me until I felt that I had entered a new world of manners where people swept through life, bowing and being bowed to, and I didn't care to go into the subject of motive too deeply at the moment, partly, perhaps, because of the obscurity of my own possible reactions.

The *maître d'hôtel,* a handsome, ceremonious sort who did as much for my ego as anyone there, gave me a table to myself, off the main dining *salon,* in a favored nook which was protected and yet had a generous view of what went on among the diners. The fact that during the first few weeks I often had to dine alone did not bother me at all for there was the exciting spectacle of the people. I was glad there were several Americans among the new faces for they would become the necessary contrast to the world I hoped to adopt. As a matter of fact, it occurred to me, they would provide me with a way of looking back, of cautiously considering the figures of an antipathetic past while I moved forward into a future defining itself more as I had dreamed. Consequently my position in the smaller dining room became one of privileged observation, an elegant echo of a fantasy I used to enjoy as a boy when I sat in the car waiting for my mother to return from shopping and watched faces, giving them names, characters, and destinies. To be able to continue this form of exploratory appraisal among people whom I might yet get to know gave me perhaps some sense of

84

progress which was one of the things I was worried about.

It was, I believe, the second day at lunch, when my focus on my surroundings was clearer and more particular, that I first noticed the old lady whom, reverting to the habit of long ago, I immediately called "the White Queen" because of her striking lordliness, the imperial manner in which she swept into the *salon,* took in everything at a glance, noting all changes, and sat down promptly in her nook within a nook, an extreme corner of the room where several ornate columns cloistered her regally without obstructing her panorama. You could see that she was an old-timer at the hotel—if there had been deference for me, there was something sacrosanct in the manner in which she was treated by the *maître d'hôtel* and the waiter. She was obviously an American, one of the whitest and oldest looking individuals I had ever seen, and it fascinated me to consider how and where all this age and powder-whiteness had come upon her and whether the secret of national senescence might not be concentrated in her, distilled, as it were, in the alembic of the tropics. Her body, surprisingly slender and springy, was not congruent with her head, giving her the look of having once been decapitated and physically refurbished with an older countenance. Her face was bound in a network of wrinkles stretching even across the nose to the ears, up to the roots of the hair, and disappearing into her dress, not particularly noticeable on her arms and hands, as though some tremendous will had stanched their further progression.

I noticed how she watched the movements of the waiter, sometimes smiling at something that pleased her. Her eyes were bright, unaged, and of as indeterminate color as those of a bird. There was a kind of dry, white effulgence emanating from her, and the lithe, dark waiter seemed a sensuous and encroaching shadow which she alternately wooed and repulsed. I saw him spill a little sugar on the table, and immediately a shrill barrage of heavily accented Portuguese came chattering out of her mouth while she began to fidget and flutter, and I characterized her as a *rara avis,* a very old, white bird of a woman sacred to herself and apparently to others. But this image did not last, for I was to see her, as I did not then know, in innumerable changes and avatars, an elusive, chameleon-form of memory and imagination. The slender shadow of the waiter bent over her, as obsequiously pliant as an overhanging tree, and the anger drained from her face, leaving it more supple with life. Then she smiled, and I could have sworn that she looked twenty years younger, so positive she was in regaining her manner and composure, looking around the room with cool arrogance like someone who had been accustomed to please. I was used to the inconstancy of the human face, my own included, a factor in the sensation of the illusory character of things I sometimes experienced (that was why, I suppose, I had become an unobtrusive starer), but I was not prepared for such variability in an old face, for, after all, I told myself, it at least should be "set."

I knew that she had been immediately aware of my presence —such eyes as hers sharpen themselves upon the minute perception of the world around them, growing keener with age—and I was certain that she glanced my way from time to time. It seemed that she looked more histrionic, more assuredly the *grande dame* at intervals during lunch, and I had a notion that it was when she was aware of my furtive scrutiny. When our eyes met first, a fleeting trace of a smile, like the condescension of royalty, passed over her face, but the second time her glance paused longer, and I felt myself completely enveloped in her concentration which broke into a freer smile, brushed with a nuance of coquettishness. She was inviting me to admire her! That I could see. The impish little albino monkey (for now that was the momentary image) was trying to radiate its force across the room in a travesty of seductiveness, commanding the blandishment of my attention. And, strangely, there was something hypnotic about her smile, charged with an old, tireless, inexhaustible habit of allurement. She believed that her beauty endured, and there was a force of memory and confidence that had never given up its transmittal. She looked younger, yes, she did, her features stimulated with intent, and it was an easy

86

thing, in the trance of a new impression, to see the face rebuild itself, like slow-motion played backwards, until she was to me something more of what her own conception might have been. It highlighted a conflict of mine to see that the way a person thought of himself, if it were dynamic enough, might partly produce the aura he walked in for others.

II

Several weeks had passed, and I had come to know the White Queen, although my understanding of her, it seemed, had scarcely begun. From my first awareness of her, I had been fascinated. She was surely one of those who had "lived"—she had something to teach me if only I could know her. There must have been a "secret" and a "struggle" in her life—her face said that—and with my old desire for penetration into human character I was determined to find out. If I discovered what her great moments had been, her crises, defeats, and victories, it might indicate to me how the graph of a human life evolved, for I was undecided about all these things.

I made discreet inquiries concerning her at the desk, among friends and even chance acquaintances with whom I had seen her talking, for her presence in the hotel was pervasive, and these facts emerged: Her name was Mrs. Edward Estlin, and she was the widow of a U. S. Steel executive. Estlin's work had kept them in Brazil for some years, and then they had left suddenly under the hushed rumor of scandal, something about a young Brazilian army officer and Mrs. Estlin. *"Une petite histoire d'amour,"* one of the Brazilian residents of the hotel told me with a twinkle in his eye. And just before the war, she had returned, "for good," so she said. "She's *muito rica*, terribly rich, you know," another Brazilian said, as though that meant wise and worthy as well.

87

I was not surprised to find the local appraisal full of deference and tolerance, for the Brazilian has more avuncular respect than the American. America is the land for the young if they know what they want, and I rather expected the boisterous Navy lieutenant to say: "Sure I know old lady Estlin. She's the one, you know, who shacked up with one of these niggers down here. With all her highfalutin' airs, just think of the old biddy doing that." And Carleton Andrews, a second-rate lecturer on America, sponsored by the Cultural Relations Office of the Embassy, told me shortly after a snub from Mrs. Estlin: "I'm leaving the Gloria. They ought to rake some of those old mummies out from behind the columns. Like that Estlin bitch. You know what she told me? Said I was doing more harm than good down here. She's a fine one to be going around putting on airs anyway. They say she liked some of these brown boys around town. Used to be a regular old whore, I hear." His story made me smile, for I could imagine her, angry, scornful, hard as an old powder horn, exploding in the face of the soft, silly Mr. Andrews who had perhaps neglected her in some way and incurred her displeasure.

But everything I heard was vague or vituperative. I looked her up in the Hotel Register and found that she had a New York address, noticing with a mixture of feelings that her apartment was directly beneath my room. Our acquaintance from day to day had grown by nods, bows, and smiles that never quite met, but I had come to want to really know her and even to like her, and I was glad when she made the first overture, stopping me as I passed her table: "Oh, this is Mr. Anthony Wilson, isn't it? Well, I'm Mrs. Estlin." She extended a hand in a quick, grasping, bird-like gesture. "I understand you're new here, and I want to get to know you. Do sit down and talk awhile." Evidently it was little girl's day somewhere in her moods, for she was dressed in a puffy, pale pink dress, and her face had been made up in a doll-like fashion.

"I'm very glad to know you, Mrs. Estlin. I've heard a lot about you," was about all I could get out before she began to play all

88

the forces of her personality upon me at once. I was amazed to find that she talked about the present constantly with only here and there a name out of the past, like a jewel suddenly turned on her nervous fingers blinding me with its associations, so that the present seemed all the more in her command. She asked me a great many questions about myself and began subtly to give me compliments, but all the time I felt she was thinking about someone else, someone she thought should exist. "The Embassy needs young men of your sort, Mr. Wilson," she would say, and I found her manner as suave as an Ambassador's wife appraising the staff. "We have so many of the wrong kind of Americans coming down here. No distinction whatever. Have you met that outrageous Mr. Andrews? Cultural Relations, indeed. He's the laughingstock of Rio." She looked cruel, feeling herself then, one could see, very much the white goddess of judgment so that all of the straining power of her wrinkles seemed to have gathered into the deep furrow between her eyebrows. But I felt that she was right. Surely she knew what Brazilians would feel, for wasn't she the oldest American in Rio, didn't she have the cumulative, backward look which was the only proper justification of authority? And I admired the conviction in her voice, the varying, mobile manifestations of herself, each assured, and her ability to imprint these impressions on me, but still I had not discovered the central source of her strength, the buoyant principle beneath all the years.

I tried to imagine what impression I had really made on her— this was very important to me. I knew I had a fine frame (over six feet tall, and strongly built—"a fine figure of a man," according to my grandmother, although it was strange how small I often felt) , there was excellent bone structure in my face, and I had a good vital crop of dark-auburn hair and soft gray eyes. This I knew from the cage of mirrors in which I lived, but there was a discrepancy somewhere, for I could never synchronize my feelings with the convergence of reflections. Each view of my physical self, which I had thought about many times, suggested something different, and its inner echo was incongruent. Now, as always, I could see myself sitting with this old but oddly changing, withered and unwithering lady, and I was attentive, complaisant, and apparently charmed, but, as nearly always, there was a shadow in the picture, something in the reflection I did not understand, as though it might be the meaning of the little scene itself, as though there were someone unknown within me who was meant to comment upon that *tête à tête* and its hanging shadow, as upon thousands of others in the past, but had never learned to speak, so this picture, like all the rest, had no name.

The luncheon finished with pleasantries, and I could see that the young, auburn-haired man had afforded the white, columnar lady a *divertissement*. I had listened for the "wheres," the "whens," the "hows," and the "whys," throughout her conversation, as I would always do. But I still had only the slightest notion of who she was. If I found out, I told myself, it would help me in some way which was still vague to me and intellectually undetermined.

When I left her, I ceased to worry about her or myself—I had gone far enough for the time being. I felt content to be the auburn-haired young man who was making friends so rapidly, who lived in a pleasant world where nothing seemed to bar his entrance. There were these momentary congruencies when the man in the mirror was myself. I looked out of the great French doors which opened on to the broad, front terrace of the hotel. The whole girth of the building was sashed in with the blue of the sea as though its impulse were toward spilling itself in the fluent motion of the water. A wind was blowing, and everything felt drawn in its current toward the funnel of the mountains at the end of the bay, and beyond was the great whorl-mouth of the open ocean. The entire city seemed to pour toward that opening where the blue nirvana of the water was waiting for us all, and I felt fluid and gliding, and the burden of longing for some stasis within was for the time lost in the swoon of that strange beckoning.

90

III

After a few weeks, the Ambassador sent me to Manaus, a lost, torpid, little town in the north of Brazil on the Amazon. I was going ostensibly to appraise the state of the Consulate there, determine the need for any further personnel, and make a report of its progress in general, but I had the feeling I was given the job because the Ambassador did not know what else to do with me at the moment. A wily, heartless old manipulator, he moved his officers into position like a chess player, and I disliked to be around him for he had the eye of a devil for what was not in a man. At any rate, I sensed that he thought I had not fitted in, or rather that he had failed with me as though an amorphous substance had eluded the mold of his hand, and that I was to be sent into the hinterlands to see Rio at a distance and know how much I should lose if I lost it permanently.

Manaus meant absolutely nothing to me until the fact that it didn't began actually to be unnerving. I went through my routine with the officials of the Consulate in a listless manner, hazily laying away certain facts to convey to the Ambassador. All was somnolence and torpor and the realization of how prone and limp man had become in such an environment. With nothing combatting the surrounding jungle, there was a prevailing atmosphere of the ancient mire of life in which it was necessary to delve one's sensations in the only discernible drive, the will to live, shared by the rest of the animal world.

I longed for Rio which, once as lush and loose as a full-blown flower, seemed now hard and white as a jewel, a diamond-center of civilization which alone could have made that jungle meaningful. An experience, more painful to me perhaps than to another, was the feeling expressed in a line remembered from Shakespeare "that wisdom cries out in the streets, and no man regards it." Truth, Honor, Justice, Love—these were words I had thought I might find a better meaning for in a foreign country, finally giving up the Service, perhaps, settling wherever I possessed the security of that knowledge. "Chalice-terms," some professor back home had called them, but here in Manaus, more than in Rio, they were as dry as empty gourds.

My friends I missed most of all, though in missing them I suppose I missed myself. I spent much of my free time away from the Consulate trying to remember them in detail and how I had been with them. The fellows at the Embassy—what did we stand for together?—Perla Azevedo, my new girl, incomparable dancer and gay companion but haunting and elusive friend. Most often of all I thought of the White Queen, for, in the weeks before I left Rio, she had forged so many images of herself upon my consciousness. I hadn't seen her for any length of time on any given occasion—there was too much divergence in our ages for that—but, daily, in passing, I met her, and with the quick power of her personality she made herself memorable. I recalled her in countless ways: as the old white bird, the impish, albino monkey, sometimes silent, hard, and ungiving as a death's head, sometimes in the old costume of what was once a *femme fatale,* she was like a yellow rose pressed at its full-blown peak in a book too many years ago. Or, in the rich pleasure of her own personality, she was often like a fountain, pluming whitely, freely, and clearly, watering the ground around it, an unflagging, abundant source of life, confounding its detractors. Or, again, upon special occasion, in another reminiscent fashion, she wore a fillet around her white curls, and she could have been, in the glow of her own illusion, Juno, Minerva, or Venus.

I wanted to believe in the best of her story, to think that she embodied a sacred nobility, that she had sacrificed herself in some passionate and beautiful ordeal. It was Love, the highest and least known to me of all the worrisome words that I wished to attach to her. She had broken her life over an impossible affair, and had left in disgrace, returning to Rio as one always wishes to return to the place where one has truly lived. I preferred to believe that until such time as her secret would be mine. Whatever doubt and discord there was in my conception,

her occasional arrogance, a sudden remark of chilling calculation, were glossed over and stored in the repository of nameless
and unspoken suppositions which I had accumulated during
the years. I knew that she had watched my appreciation grow
and was pleased as a clever teacher might have been with an
indulgent and willing pupil. Often, as we became less formal,
she watched my eyes intently when I seemed to be dreaming in
her presence, and I knew she was aware of their gray vacuity as
though they might be filled with various sorts of soul. "Ah, Mr.
Wilson," she would say. "You have the eyes of a dreamer. Be
careful. Don't let yourself be the prey of the dreamless."

I finished my work in Manaus as rapidly as possible, the report
comfortably couched in its Departmental clichés, and was on
my way back. The coming reunion with my friends promised a
true rehabilitation. I could see them coming to meet me, bringing back things I had lost. "Oh, Tony, you have been away so
long," Perla would say, returning to me the motion and manners of our relationship until I was once again myself mixed
with Perla. "Tell me all about it," she would continue, and I
would have the thrilling sensation so rare for me that she also
sought to recapture some part of herself. And the fellows at the
Embassy would ask me about the trip jocosely, scornfully, or
enviously, and perhaps they would reveal what there was that
was new in me. But Mrs. Estlin would be the center of the
return for, whereas Manaus was without age and without
humanity, she was full of the years of man, and I looked forward to our reunion, for I felt that there was still so much to
be learned from her.

The plane was late, and we got into Rio long after dark, but
I could sense the city powerfully beneath me, the strings of
light like little, pulsing, jewel-dynamos of its life, and all the
tentacles of my sensation spread out to embrace it. Tomorrow
there would be once again the old, recovered life with its new
accretions yet to be claimed from the recognition of others. As
I thought of the new blending of myself with the old associations, I felt an odd mixture of feelings welling up in me again:

the longing to "stay" and the longing to "go." In the morning, there would be the view of the sea from the Hotel and the winds and their nisus toward the channel of the mountains, the throat of the cornucopia which poured its faces and figures, like blossoms and fruits, into blue nothingness beyond. Yet something in me, a ghost of the real, would be standing on the terrace with waving hand, incurved, saying: "Wait, wait," even as now my hands grasped the arms of the seat in the silver plane that was falling like a bauble into that braided flow of pleasure and regret.

After a light snack in town, for I knew that the dining room at the Gloria would be closed, I went directly to the Hotel and prepared for bed. As I lay down, I felt turbulent with memories of Manaus, what I had probably missed, remembering the irony of my disinterest while I was there. I was disturbed with the fact that at least parts of my experience seemed to have no value until they were past or until they had been recreated or given substance by the relating of them to others. What would happen as time passed if, habituated to recall as the necessary matrix of the emergence of that mythic being of strength, wisdom, and beauty which was always yet to be born in me, I could no longer draw assurance of its manifold nature, its inevitable coming, from those around me who had always been its heralds and perhaps the masks of its soul? Had I not always believed, like Joyce's Stephen Dedalus, that I desired "to press in my arms the loveliness which has not yet come into the world"? Or, was this only a way of telling myself the romance of things I would never do?

It was an unusually hot, still night, and I found I could not sleep. Since the forms of things were submerged in darkness, I decided, as I had often done before, to interest myself in the sounds of life with that sensuous avidity which had never forsaken me. On this particular night, my room seemed a very high perch, as though I were in a tree-house, and I could hear the night-birds close by, outside the window, and breathing up like a slow exhalation (since there was no wind) was the never-to-be-forgotten smell of the hill behind the Hotel, its jungle-nature only half-concealed—it was the scent of root, lubricant dampness, and the voluptuous earth. A part of me sensed the pungent presence like the dark form of a lover, but something else cried out, "Is this, then, all?"

I was distracted from my causerie with the night by one of the sounds of life I had been wooing. I thought there was an animal in the woods nearby at first. It was a strange crooning, like a muttering of witchcraft from some dark cave. I lay quite still until I realized that it was the sound of a human voice and that it came from the room directly beneath mine.

When the tremor of surprise cleared from my mind, for I had never before heard a single sound emerging from below, until it had, indeed, become for me a "secret chamber," I heard a voice speaking in a mixture of English and Portuguese which seemed to increase its wantonness: *"Meu amor,* my love, my love. You're a beauty, *uma beleza.* Never forget that . . . never, never forget that. . . . Look how the young American beats his wings around you, *meu amor,* my beauty. Like Edward before he started to forget . . . Edward who would have forgotten, my beauty, until you taught him to remember with Armando. Ah, Armando who broke his heart for you, my beauty. Who cried and wished to kill himself because you did not love him. But he was like an empty gun in your hand, of no use any more, so what could you do, *meu amor,* my love? . . . But still they come, these Brazilians, dark, ugly, loathsome . . . but still they come. The flower still has its perfume. . . . The Americans neglect you, eh? . . . but, ah, there is Mr. Wilson . . . have you not captured his soul, my beauty? Is he not yours, my love?"

There was a sound of hands that were patting and pummeling flesh, and I could imagine her seated at her boudoir table in a cosmetic ritual, the ceremony of mummification long drawn out through all the years. The lamp would accentuate the whiteness with all corrosive rouge and paint removed, the cleansing tissue lying about like blood-smeared rags, and there she sat, unrelenting and supreme, the sovereign of her long and savage "struggle." Her room, I thought, if only she could see it, was hung with nothing but masks of victims, death's-heads of all the selves which she had killed.

Next morning I moved to another floor on the other side of the Hotel with the idea of changing permanently to the Copacabana as soon as it was feasible. No one could deny that it was a more beautiful hotel or that it could offer me more in the long run. It was full of glitter and grace, a center of youth and endless activity and, perhaps, I would find an answer there for all my foolish indecisions. I remembered the elegant salons full of mirrors, and I could see myself there in the evening, dressed in my best for dancing, with Perla, white-gowned and shining in diamonds, the two of us together, walking quickly along as though life had no end of brilliance.

THE CITY
OF ALL THE SAINTS

THE PLANE FROM RIO WAS LATE, AND PERHAPS THE flight to São Salvador would be canceled. It would probably be better that way, Nathan reflected. He could get along without them. There was Dona Helena, who spoke English well enough to substitute for Mrs. Velma in conversation; Nelson Esteves could pinch-hit for Reed Daniels in the modern poetry course; and he could surely find someone else around to take over grammar for Dunstan Pennypacker. And, of course, there would be Amelia to help with the social side.

If they came, they would be the first Americans he had seen officially in a long time, and they were always so much worse that way. It would be quite a *coup* to at least start without them and show he could manage the summer session of English classes alone. The Embassy had more or less crammed them down his throat anyway, and the director of the Associacão Cultural had not backed him up. He was a little ashamed about his feelings, but it was true, he didn't meet Americans very easily any more. There were so few of them in Bahia. Even the War hadn't brought them at first, but now they would be coming abundantly in the name of culture.

Well, if they must, why didn't they get it over with? An about-to-be-pounced-on feeling hovered over the little airport such as a savage might have had from some ill omen in the sky. He went outside and stood in the gentle sunshine, remembering what one of his friends had said: "The light in Bahia has soft fingers." His eyes moved toward his reflection in the big glass window as though the caressive sensation could be seen as well as felt.

Several Brazilians were standing near him, and he noticed pleasurably that he could easily be taken for one of them. With his close-cropped, dark hair, brown eyes and skin, and his short stature, he flowed with the mass of the nation, dressed like most of them in a white suit and heavy thick-soled shoes like moorings of the buoyant flesh. And, there was no doubt about it, he was thinner, though he ate voraciously as his physicality seemed to grow more porous. But he was slender like the stalk of a plant before it bursts into heady bloom, his face relaxed and luminous as though the air had been buffing it with oil. A friend at Harvard had told him once that he had a face like Kafka's, but that look of a mask jutting through a tympanum of nerves was surely gone.

Another anxious glance at the sky spotted a dark, wing-shaped blot, premonitive as the image of a bat. As it drew nearer, it looked uglier and more rapacious, not belonging to the old city of Bahia at all, and Nathan wished that nature could have responded with the rending sound of a web of gold being torn when the plane plunged down through the mesh of soft, radiant air, finally grounding itself, a wounded, metallic bird that ejected passengers like throttled flesh through a cleft in armor.

There was a fussy-looking young man with a moustache, who must be Dunstan Pennypacker, then a dark line of Brazilians followed by an American woman, nondescriptly pretty, surely Mrs. Velma, another garrulous chain of *bahianos,* then another American, a tall, good-looking fellow, coming out last like the one who had really brought them there, pausing at the top of the stairs as they do in the newsreel. That, of course, would be Reed Daniels.

Nathan shook hands all around, extended the Associação's welcome, trying to achieve the easy informality of such occasions at home—it was up to him to take over now. Jamming the group together into the taxi, he repacked them as quickly as

100

possible before they spread out from the tight constriction of their journey too loosely and pervasively.

"It's a several mile drive into town," he explained. "You'll see why when we get there. It's all up and down hill."

"Oh," Daniels said. "That will be interesting. I like to see what sort of landscape surrounds a city. I have a feeling there's always a connection, an accommodation or a rebellion of one sort or another." There was something in his voice which lured Nathan to turn from his position by the driver and look him in the face. "You might as well know, Mr. Kinberg," he went on, "we're really worked up about our visit, and are counting on you to show us around. After all, we're just Rio hicks. This is our first trip away, and it's about time we knew something about the rest of Brazil."

"There'll be plenty of chance for that. We have classes only in the morning," Nathan said.

"Except for you," Daniels continued with a smile. "Remember, we're students too, the subject, Bahia. *A cidade de todos os santos,* the city of all the saints—isn't that what they used to call it?"

"Yes. There's supposedly a church for every day of the year. I don't know that anyone's ever bothered to count them."

"But who was it, then, that called it *a terra violenta?*"

"Jorge Amado, I believe. Whether you'll see that side depends on you. Most tourists never do." Maybe that would shut him up for a while. The easy charm had begun to be annoying. Why did some people have to try to sound so "interested"?

But he was not to be let off that easily. As soon as Daniels stopped talking, Pennypacker started in, chattering continuously as they drove into town, mainly, one could see, as an entertainment for Daniels. He was not going to be a problem but an annoyance, something you would want to brush away rather than bothering to kill. The talk was mainly of Mrs. Velma's airsickness, and there again the picture was clear: Daniels sitting beside her, consoling her, providing irrefutable proof of

101

human health and constancy, and the high, thin voice of Penny-packer rising like the fumes of her discomfort. Nathan disliked her even more than Daniels—she had the kind of supine femininity he simply couldn't abide. Daniels had already conquered her without trying, that was evident, and, most probably, though not a trouble maker, she would turn out to be a deadly bore.

It was amazing how in a few minutes they had completely changed his mood. On the way to the airport he had struck up an easy conversation with Pericles, the taxi driver, who had begun to tell him an uproarious story about a *morena* he had slept with the night before, describing her "cinder-shaking movement," and the car had rolled lazily along filled with a rich, warm sense of personality. But now there was an atmosphere of compulsive living; purpose and energy throbbed around him on all sides. He noticed that his countrymen, all soap, perfume, shaving lotion, and dry-cleaned clothes, even smelled aggressively different from Pericles who gave off a nutty, earthy blend of coffee, tobacco, and clothes so accommodated to human sweat that they no longer smelt stale.

He tried to be what he knew they were expecting of him, the genial guide who understood both sides of everything, but the words wouldn't come. Without comment he let the landscape fly by in streamers while Pericles, harshly silent, eyed him like a stranger. It occurred to him that, though he was ostensibly in command, of all the people in the car his life force was the most muted, deflected erratically from its new bed by some unexpected resurgence of a primal source.

When he had deposited them at the only hotel in town, a gray, characterless structure, indifferent about its bad food and hard beds—a vengeful insult to the intruder—Nathan shook hands again, promising to come by at ten in the morning to show them the town before classes began the next day. As he walked home alone, he felt the "American feeling" inside him again. He had been a heel, officially polite, of course, but it was the colorless kind of greeting he might have given a salesman.

102

Nobody had called him Jew-boy, and yet he was acting like the son of old Jake Kinberg who ran a junkyard in Brooklyn, the bitter young man who had shoved off for Brazil a year before the War to get away from it all.

Stopping by his favorite bar, he called for a shot of *cachaça* and pineapple juice and sat down at his regular table, sipping the sweet, slowly burning drink in the ripe, fruity atmosphere of the rum-scented room. All of his plans had gone wrong. He was going to be superior to the situation, he was not going to let them know whether he cared if they were around or not. He was going to be so friendly to them that they wouldn't be able to get anywhere near him. But they had turned out to be a bunch of Jew-lovers, which was as bad as the other thing. They were the "new" American; they overlooked your race like a gift they were giving you. You could see how good it made them feel. Especially Daniels. He was a benign son of a bitch if there ever was one.

Leaving the bar without his usual second drink, he was glad to reach his apartment, for nothing in it reminded him of home. There were no photographs, no homey objects, but voodoo baubles and *escola da Bahia* paintings hanging on the walls, and many plants and flowers, so profuse in places one felt that the earth had burst through—its smell was everywhere like the trapped breath of growth. But, as his mood shifted again, its blandishments seemed dead. What was wrong with him anyway? These people couldn't knock the funnel of plenty from his lips even if they tried. It was he, not they, who had been in São Salvador for four years; this was his bailiwick, not theirs. He was set for the duration or as long thereafter as he wanted to remain. Hadn't the Embassy declared him "essential" and Bahia called him "desirable"? God damn them all. Why couldn't they stay in Rio where they belonged with the rest of the invaders and opportunists?

When he finally went to bed, the deep, dreamless, inactive sleep of the tropics which had become his, the sleep of things growing outside, waiting for the sunlight, evaded him. Slipping

103

on a light robe, for he slept without pajamas now, having recovered his nakedness, he got up and strolled into the garden. The night was thick and close, lacking the far, starlit purity of the North, brushing against the skin like the moist pelt of an animal. As always, the air was saturated with mysterious essences, so laden with pollen that the earth seemed to be planting itself in the flesh. When he paused in an arbor of trees, the still, murky green encircled him like a diver's bell until the thread of the cricket's voice pulsed nearby. It was always a haunting effect, this still and then throbbing darkness whose only message was that of generation: sire and conceive, sire and conceive. But it disturbed him for he felt that he had lost its rhythm, and, though alerted on all sides by the sounds of the night, he prowled numbly around the garden as if he looked for the bones of someone he had buried.

Morning was a yellow-orange exhalation of the earth with a tang in the air, not winey as in cold climates, but still streaked by the dark's residual musk. It stirred the physical first, and there was a feeling of left-over hunger needing the pith of all nourishment to sate it. Nathan felt much better, as though the day had raked through his flesh and turned it like soil to the sun. Keep on good turns with yourself, boy, he thought, as he shaved. Easy does it. Remember this is *boa terra*. They'll never be able to do anything about that.

In a way, he had to admit a part of him was secretly glad to see some Americans. It had something to do perhaps with "catching up on the news." Even if you didn't like them, they knew a lot of things you knew. He remembered that Gertrude Stein said the U.S.A. was her country though Paris was her home. Well, he felt like that about Bahia. In spite of how much he loved foreigners they always suggested the theatrical, as though the life they lived was not quite real and you would one day have to step outside and see what was really going on, and that would be the day you remembered you were an American. Knowing this, he sometimes felt like a character from one of

104

Somerset Maugham's tropic stories who had and had not given up. These people coming in on him represented law and order; they were from the truant office back home. All that he needed to do, though, was to make them enter the play, draw them into the story, and force them to accept the illusion, if such it was.

When he arrived at the hotel, the Americans were waiting for him in the lobby. It would have been better to have seen them singly the first time, but, no matter, his sense of dissolvent calm was equal to the occasion. Once again, Reed Daniels stood out among them, distinct between the limp dependency of Mrs. Velma and the fluttery nervousness of Pennypacker. He had brown hair and gray eyes, but the over-all impression was somehow blond; there seemed to be tides of light moving under his skin which never quite broke through the surface.

Nathan took them down into the lower city first to see the gay little boats with their forest of masts. Then they passed on through the open markets, full of squatting figures lumped together with fruits, fish, and vegetables for sale. He tried to make it seem as leisurely as possible for that was the effect he wanted to convey.

"That's the *vestimenta bahiana* we've heard so much about, isn't it, Nathan?" Daniels asked as a group of Negro women passed, wearing gaudy turbans, long white blouses, necklaces of coral, turquoise, ivory and silver, and bright ballooning skirts where their slender bodies hung like clappers in huge many-colored bells.

"Yes," Nathan said. "They got the idea from the hoop skirt of colonial times. Sort of like the Southern slave who wanted to look like the mistress of the Big House." He could have gone on and told them a lot, but decided he could wait.

"Well, I think they're simply divine, Dr. Kinberg," Mrs. Velma said airily. "I'm just crazy about all that color. Wouldn't you love to have something like that to wear at a costume party back home?"

"No, I don't think so, Mrs. Velma. Not on Mr. Kinberg. I hardly think he's the type. Not even on Halloween." Pennypacker twitched his little moustache and beamed at Daniels for approval.

"Why, Dr. Pennypacker. Did I say *him?* Well, you know I meant *me.*" She turned to Nathan. "He's such a tease, Dr. Kinberg. He just didn't give me a moment's peace all the way up."

Daniels had walked on ahead and was looking up at the older part of the city which loomed above them like an irregular patchwork crown of stone. They took the big town-elevator and went up to the main square and then into the streets, laid out often as not in the pattern of vines. The houses were low and softly colored and, when inhabited, smelled of cooking food, musky flesh, and flowers, a peculiarly sensual blend, Daniels decided, the "scent of the tropics." Rising like handles of the many hills were the churches with pyramiding, scrolled, and blue-tiled towers. *"A cidade de todos os santos,"* he said. "I haven't seen anything to compare with it anywhere else. The concentration is simply terrific, particularly for this climate."

"If you like baroque," Pennypacker sniffed. "A little of it goes a long way with me."

"It's not the architectural style so much, Dunstan. It's the effort."

"You're so right, Dr. Daniels," Mrs. Velma chimed in. "Why to see all of those people lying around down there in the market limp as rags you'd never think they'd ever get up and do anything like this."

"Well, I guess they got religion all right. But it didn't last long. Look at them now," Pennypacker said, moving along impatiently.

"Oh, I wouldn't say that, Dunstan. These things go in cycles, you know. Wait a hundred years."

"That suits me fine, starting tomorrow. But let's get going now. There may be plenty of the old-time religion around, but this sun is as hot as Hades."

Nathan let them talk, seldom joining in, now tense in spite of himself, watching carefully for every reaction. He had acquired the cicerone's desire to impress his audience—they must

106

somehow see the old city through his eyes. Mercilessly pushing on, he took them up and down the deserted, mouldering streets with grass growing between the cobblestones, the open gutters like runnels of dissolution, a downhill wash so apparent in places that the city seemed to be sloughing off into a gulch of earth.

But as the morning wore on he felt the tarnishing influence of the others begin to depress him. What he was trying to give them was an intimacy that would explain his devotion, but he increasingly got the impression that they were taking mental notes and photographs with the traveler's materialism which afflicted so many Americans. Of course, it wasn't exactly fair to think that, considering how generous their enthusiasm was on the whole. Maybe it was just that the old city wasn't so wonderful after all. Perhaps he was beginning to see it through their eyes in spite of himself. He began to feel entirely too much "on location," having, ironically enough, entrusted himself with giving them a close-up of a city that didn't exist at all.

When Mrs. Velma finally complained of hunger, he forced the appreciation of a final scene and led them down on the wharf again to a second-story café where only *comida bahiana* was served. Crammed together in a small, hot, noisy, odorous room, their bodies felt like fat kernels of flesh after the wistful loneliness of the outer streets.

"By the way, Nathan," Pennypacker said, as though he closed a book of the morning's tour and opened another more interesting one which he had been reading. "I'd like to ask you if we're supposed to use any Portuguese in our classes. I've found that it sometimes helps. If they can't get an idiomatic phrase in English, I just pop in the Portuguese equivalent, and they learn it just like that. Saves a lot of time I've found."

"I'd like to know about that too," Mrs. Velma broke in. She was sagging and frazzled from the walk in the sun, but her basic prettiness, like a child's, couldn't be done away with. "You see, I'm not very good at Portuguese. I was talking to Dr. Daniels about that on the plane and he seemed to think—"

107

"Well, you don't have to worry about that," Nathan interrupted. "A lot of the students in the classes are men. Even if you make a mistake, they'd never let you know." He might have trouble with this silly woman after all. She'd be a pushover if anything in pants took after her.

"Make them like the subject and they'll learn," he went on more sociably. "The Bahiano is very agreeable, very courtly. He wants to like you if you'll let him. Just don't be too strict, and don't be so friendly that they don't know who's boss. They like to be managed a bit. It makes them feel that you know what you're doing." He glanced at Pennypacker who was fidgeting with displeasure. If given a chance, the dreary little fool would turn the luncheon into a seminar.

"Well, I don't agree, Nathan. I think the teacher should use Portuguese from time to time if he can use it correctly," he said, looking at Mrs. Velma condescendingly. "I've found the student has more respect for a man who can speak his language."

"Don't you think it depends on the individual?" Daniels asked, planting himself so easily in the middle of the seesaw that Mrs. Velma smiled at him gratefully. "Good teaching is pretty much a matter of personality. We all have to do it differently. I know my Portuguese isn't what it should be either." He turned away from the others and Nathan thought he detected a glimmer of amusement in his eyes. "I think Nathan's right. The important things for the teacher to remember are humility and the wish to communicate. None of us will get anywhere if we aren't *simpático*."

Nathan almost felt friendly toward him for a moment, but then recoiled. Those weren't exactly his words, but coming from Daniels it sounded like perhaps what he had meant to say. If the man was wooing him as he did the others, he was not to be had! But when he contrived a reason for seeing something in the other viewpoint, Pennypacker took the opportunity of leading them all down a long hall of pedantry, his voice buzzing like a hummingbird, until Nathan groaned at the result of his own treachery. It was the kind of "how many angels can dance on the head of a pin" mentality which he had met so often at Harvard.

Fortunately the *vatajá* came, highly peppered and fused into congealed flame. While the others tasted it gingerly, Nathan consumed great quantities with chauvinistic gusto, taking a secret pleasure in watching the little beads of sweat form on Mrs. Velma's brow while she ate with tight-closed mouth as though smoke or steam might billow through her teeth.

When he took them back to the hotel, they all looked done in. Damn it, what was he trying to prove? He couldn't let go, he had to show them every god-damned thing in town. They'd gang up on him for sure now. That little son of a bitch Pennypacker was already acting up.

He stopped in a *botequim* and went behind the counter to telephone.

"Hello? Amelia? What's doing tonight?" He waited for the pleasurable little feminine gurgle to bubble in his ears. "Good. See you about eight then, *meu bem.*"

Well, that was that. Damned if he was going to have dinner with them. They could rot in that stinking hotel until they showed a little more interest. Let them find their own way around from now on. If he changed his mind, he could drop by the hotel with Amelia and they could all have a drink together in the bar. Maybe that would be a better way of showing them he had what he wanted.

Four weeks of the Summer School went by and the students agreed that it was the best session they could remember. There was no doubt that much of the credit belonged to the Americans, and Daniels had made a particular hit. His modern poetry course was refreshingly *contra-clássico,* heady and exciting after Longfellow and Poe who were the only American poets most of them knew. Once, Nathan, pausing in the hall to eavesdrop, heard the class reading Amy Lowell's "Lilacs" together, chanting the lines along with Daniels, and the sound streamed over him like a strange draught of America and Brazil flowing together.

Even Dona Rogeria, the oldest of the teachers, finally succumbed, treating Daniels like a kind of new embodiment of Nathan so that her original allegiance might be kept intact. The unmarried women constantly gossiped in the halls about the young professor and began to bring him little gifts: a good luck *figa* for his watch chain, ash trays of painted shell, and a beautiful wood carving of a saint. One day, after class, when Nathan saw him sitting at his desk which was littered with trinkets, he was infuriated and thought of an excuse to speak to him.

"That's a good outline you posted on the bulletin board," he said. "But I was surprised to see you were doing T. S. Eliot, Wallace Stevens, and Hart Crane. Don't you think they're a little difficult for foreign language students?"

Daniels looked up good-humoredly. How was it that he looked so casual and so thoroughly in command of the situation at the same time? He had been teaching all morning, and yet there he sat in his linen suit, fresh and unruffled, managing to look so much "whiter" than anyone else.

"Yes, that's true," he said. "But I don't see how I can do it any other way. You can't do Frost, Robinson, and Sandburg, and leap over to Millay and a few of the easier ones at the end. This is a mature group of English teachers after all. But sit in on the course for a while if you like, Nat, and then see what you think. I'd like to get your reactions."

He got up and smiled disarmingly, stretching himself. "How about a game of tennis this afternoon? I hear you're pretty good. I'm only a duffer myself, but I'd like to take you on anyway."

"You're giving me my choice of weapons?" Nathan asked wryly. "Well, all right. Better make it about five though. It's pretty hot."

"And so are you, I fear, my boy, and so are you. See you this afternoon."

Daniels beat him easily, almost apologetically, for the court had never been so wide to Nathan, and he just couldn't seem

110

to run for the ball. If Daniels had only crowed a bit, it would have made things better, but he gave him the kind of courtesy deal he would have given a Radcliffe freshman.

That evening he had a date with Amelia, and exploded to her.

"I'm not going to take it any more. I can't stand his arrogance any longer. I'm going to tell him where to head in."

"Why do you let it worry you, *meu querido?* Life's too short," Amelia said, quoting the cliché Americanism soothingly. She spoke like that all the time, so, though her English was fluent, she never seemed to be actively thinking in it, passing out the ready-made sayings effortlessly. Even in her own language, he had noticed, she was given to aphorisms, never questioning an authority that came to her so painlessly.

He glared at her, remembering that she had a class with Daniels. "So you've fallen under his spell, too?"

She didn't answer, but came over and kissed him, forcing him to enfold her, lingering at his lips as though she withdrew some poison that had been coming out as words. She wore a filmy magenta dress exploiting her latest penchant for overdressing, and her heavy perfume came out of its folds as from the convolutions of a voluptuous flower. Though she claimed to be pure Portuguese of "four hundred years' descent," an Indian strain was apparent in her and even a dusky negroid undertone, but none of these struggled for ascendancy, so that her breeding seemed well-kneaded by time. With her soft oval face, round dark eyes, pleasantly curved body, and thick, luxuriant hair, she suggested a fecund animal vitality.

He kissed her again. "I'm sorry, darling. I was rotten to you. I certainly make you pay."

"What you get for nothing isn't worth the asking."

"Oh you and your proverbs!" He smiled at her and rumpled her hair which fell about his hand like the rich stuff of her submission, and they sat down on the sofa and made love in earnest. He knew again that she was the only woman who had given him exactly what he wanted. All that business about soul and spirit that he had been brought up on was nothing but romantic rot.

111

What he wanted was her *life;* she fed him with feminine nourishment as he had never been fed before.

When it was over, she went back into the kitchen and got
them some refreshment, a ginger ale for him and a grape soda
for herself, humming contentedly as she poured them out. It
suddenly irritated him to see her go so easily from one physical
process to another.

"What are you purring about?" he asked apropos of nothing
but the desire to prod her apparently invulnerable sense of well-
being.

"Why, you, *meu querido.* Stroke the pussycat and she purrs,"
she answered without rancor as she passed him a sugar cookie.

But then he picked at her until he had assembled enough unpleasant little subjects to arouse her—the cheap pocket book in
English she had been reading, the oversize amethyst brooch she
wore between her breasts like a purple plum, the length of her
hair. Then deviously he led the conversation back to Daniels,
quarreling with her on the basis of the merest suspicion, pouring the unpurged spleen of the afternoon into the capacious
receptacle of her personality.

Even while he was attacking her, she seemed to sense that he
was beginning to feel better, finally daring to cower against his
side like a soft, sensitive little animal during a thunderstorm.
Then she gave him a series of goodnight kisses before taking him
to the door, letting him out with her favorite saying, *"Amanhã
tem mais."*

Walking along, he laughed softly to himself as he let the English translation slide pleasurably through his mind. "There's
more tomorrow." What a girl Amelia was! She had him where
the hair was short. There was no doubt about it. And all the
Americans in the world wouldn't be able to take that little
fleshpot away from him.

A few days later, near the end of the term, Daniels invited
him to go for an afternoon swim, and Nathan thought that this
finally was to be a showdown. But Daniels met him on the beach

casually and cordially although, as he had suspected, Penny-packer and Mrs. Velma hadn't been asked along. Thank God, the air had been purified of them. The conflict was naked and acknowledged at last but he cringed inside, recalling the oppressive atmosphere of the hayloft where two boys showed the secrets of their flesh. But Daniels seemed unaware of the tensions of the situation. It was a fine afternoon for the beach, the water green-yellow with the sun and earth, and he lounged comfortably in the sand, asking questions about the trees and flowers which grew along the bank like a bright fringe of things he didn't know. Nathan became swollen with waiting, for he could not believe that this relaxation was anything but feigned.

Finally Daniels said, "I've been meaning to ask you, Nathan, about your plans for after the War. I know you'll be here until then. And you should. You've been doing a wonderful job." He continued slowly, looking at him obliquely. "Maybe you don't know what a grand director of the Associacão you've made, but what I've heard from the students would make your ears burn. They'd like for you to stay permanently, of course, but I've been wondering if you've been giving it any thought, and just what your plans are."

"Sure. I've thought about it," Nathan said, wary of what was coming.

"Well, I don't mean to poke into your business, but what I'm getting around to asking is, are you planning to go back to the States?"

"Why? I've been happy here." If there was anything he hated it was a missionary—he would not have thought that even of Daniels.

"Oh, I don't know—mind you, I don't want to butt in if you've made your decision—but, for the sake of argument though, let's say I'm trying to talk perhaps like the other side of your own thinking. You'll have finished your work here soon. Don't you think it'll be time for you to move on then?"

"Move on by going back?" Nathan asked, his eyes contracting in the sunlight.

"No, not at all. Moving on past the old limits, I mean." He turned to Nathan impulsively. "Look here, I don't want to sound like a preacher. You've got a perfectly fine life here, but I have an idea you might be cut out for something else. This is a wonderful old city, and anybody could profit by spending a while here. But it's a long pause in time. It doesn't belong to the Twentieth Century."

"That's why I like it," Nathan said. "Hemingway's wrong. There are some islands left and I've found one."

"But it won't work. You can't just bury yourself alive."

"Who has? Just look around you, Daniels. Can you honestly say you've ever known a more beautiful and restful place?"

"No. But that's not the point. Somehow I can't see it. Your ending up as just a sun-worshipper, beachcomber—call it whatever you like."

"Well that's where you're wrong. Maybe I'm just a nature-boy at heart. All I know is that I breathe easily, eat well, sleep well, have no enemies, and if I stay here long enough, I may learn what happiness is, not just the taking of it, which is what I have longed for all my life, but the giving of it."

"But wouldn't it mean more if you didn't have to do it under glass?"

"Perhaps. But I wonder. I tried it the other way. Anyhow I'm pretty much out of touch with things back home."

"That's just the point," Daniels said enthusiastically. "I think I might be able to help you there. Maybe I didn't tell you, but I have an appointment as Assistant Prof at Harvard effective as soon as the Embassy will release me. I could put in a good word for you on a fellowship if you like."

"Well, I don't know—" Nathan began, wrinkling his brow.

"Think it over," Daniels broke in. "A matter like that can't be decided overnight. It has to seem like the right thing to do." He got up. "I think I'll go down for a dip. Join me?" But he didn't wait for an answer, and Nathan leaned back on his elbows and watched him go plunging down the beach.

As he dived in, shot from the sling of his own elasticity, and

114

re-emerged, shunting the water from his body, he was a taunting image. Nathan had had to grant him all the superficial
attributes: good looks, charm, the successful air, and now he
had been forced to discover that the man had a heart as well.
The realization that the other had "everything" came to him
with resignation as he once had accepted the fact that he had
"nothing." Lying in the sand, feeling ineluctably lonely, like a
garment of shadow discarded by the other on the way down to
the water, he saw the young American as one who seemed to be
constantly finding fresh embodiments of himself. It was overpoweringly true that they were alike, at least up to a point.
They were both "sensitives." One of the attractive things about
Daniels was his awareness, his interest in everything, all that
Nathan himself loved so much—the trees, the flowers, the beauty
of the landscape, the people—he, too, could "become" the thing
he contemplated. But from there on, something else took place.

Nathan pondered this distinction, remembering that when
he entered a flower, it became a cave and he lay there slumbering. The royal palm was a totem pole of green requiring his
submission or a tower of malachite whose immurement admitted no escape, the hibiscus a pink mouth that swallowed him
whenever he gave it a moment of his love. People, too, had
become like trees, plants, flowers—the white face, a white lily,
the darker one a blossom of another passion, the mulatto a
flower of gold and brown—this body like a vine, that a swollen
tuber, and there was a wind of acceptance blowing over all,
whispering of no other nirvana than this.

Daniels, however, had his lingering in things as they are, but
he moved on after a while. The tent of every flower, tree, or
human personality was only temporary shelter for him—he slept
or dreamt there for a moment and was on his way. As he saun-
tered along, the world would caress, entreat, or attempt to
restrain him, but he would always disentangle himself. And the
hands would let him go, as though even nature itself loved the
exploratory heart and matched its valor with miraculous coun-
terparts. Yes, Nathan had it at last, it was Daniels' sense of the

115

periphery of the real, his halo of the unrealized mystery that made him what he was.

On the eve of the departure of the Americans, after an almost tearful farewell assembly with the students, Nathan took them to a *candomblé,* for vestiges of his defensive love were still left, and this was something he thought they should see.

A desolate feeling over their leaving had gradually begun to come over him, making him think of them as people he had known. Already in his mind he composed letters to them, full of explanation of all the things he had not been able to convey. Reconsidering them romantically, he hung the nudity of his harsh judgment with concealing drapes, letting their figures roam about in his feelings at will. There were certain corners of the town which already their images seemed to haunt, and, of course, the Associacão would never again belong to him alone.

All of this he remembered as their guide drove them into a secret part of the jungle country. When the car could go no further, they went on foot for about half an hour, the difficulty of approach along a steep, stony path through the dense night increasing their expectancy. Soon they heard the monotonous throbbing of the drums, an even pressure of sound swelling the pouch of darkness.

In a candle-lit, palm-thatched shack the voodoo ritual was approaching climax. The *pae de santo,* a tall, lean, muscular man, exhorted the chosen to yield themselves to the *orixás,* working for possession of one of the sons or daughters. The men flung their arms up in the air or bolted up from the ground like an emission of the crowd, and the fat negresses moaned and shuddered beneath the cascading eruption of feeling. As Nathan explained to them, for every saint in the Catholic Church there had been found a kindred deity in the old mythology: *Xangö, Oxun, Anamburucú, Yanson.* "The Church doesn't care," he said, "as long as they come to mass. Some of the priests believe in the *candomblé* themselves. After all, you can't blame them.

116

They have it in their blood. It's the religion beneath religion."

"Yes, perhaps," Daniels said. "But it's terrible to think that this morning they were saying their 'Ave Marias.' "

"If you ask me," Pennypacker snorted, "all they want is a big jolt. And, boy, are they getting it! Feel like jumpin' in there and cuttin' a rug with 'em myself."

One of the women was "taken," falling in a swoon with eyeballs turned. Two men hauled her away to the sacred hut to lie in a trance and the exorcism continued with sprinkling of water on the ground and the casting down of seed. Others jammed into the little shanty until it seemed that a noose was tightening around the walls, tying the struggling bodies into a throbbing whole.

Mrs. Velma began to boil over.

"Oh, Dr. Kinberg, this is simply terrific," she cried. "It's just like the darkies getting religion at home. It always works me up. I declare, you'd better get me away from here soon, or I'll be down there rolling too!"

"It almost sends you, doesn't it?" Nathan said, laughing excitedly. "Those drums really beat you to a pulp."

He looked at his companions—they were worked up, they were not as far from being taken as they thought. He knew that they shared with him the quickening breath, the tumid feeling of life. They, too, had drunk the blood of the goat. Even Daniels was affected and in tune. Nathan handed him a cup of the communal *cachaça* that was being passed around, and he took a token sip. But when the air grew more fetid and close, as if the turning and twisting of the bodies had cast up a kind of smoke, he stepped back, looking remote and whiter than ever before, standing at the far edge of the circle like an idol toward which the orgy worked, beyond the haze of conception. God damn him, Nathan thought, and would have liked to leap upon him and tumble him down into the turmoil of noise and motion.

It had reminded him curiously of years ago in the shower room of the high school after gym class when the boys indulged

117

in horseplay, popping each other with towels. But there was one boy who stood aloof from it all and whom no one dared to touch. He was the biggest boy and also the best athlete in the class, full of assurance beyond his years, emanating his superiority casually like a man among adolescents, and Nathan had revered and hated him.

On the way back to the car, Mrs. Velma and Pennypacker walked ahead limply together though Pennypacker's voice still droned on like a tired little gnat. In the early morning light the growth-tangle loomed clearer, fitting images to the feel of the thongs of grass and branches that slapped them gently on all sides. They could see the bright red cones of the banana hanging down almost grossly and the fern-mat of the forest floor which stretched out endlessly around them like a brutal invitation to lie down forever. But, as he walked along silently with Daniels, Nathan felt exhilarated and keyed-up—he had not been released, he had been awakened. The tread of his feet brought "contact" again, and the mild flagellation of the brush was the kind of caressive evidence that he longed for.

Yet he knew that with the others it was different. Mrs. Velma and Pennypacker were tired; they had had quite a bang. But all that had happened to them before was so much more important than tonight. Tomorrow they would wake up in focus again. All her life Mrs. Velma would be looking for towers of strength to lean against, and Pennypacker, of course, would count those angels on the head of a pin sooner or later.

But Daniels, who said nothing now, was another matter. From time to time, a rut threw one against the other, jolting them, and they made strange friction together, walking mainly apart through the morning that did not want to come. Nathan's wavering new feeling of friendship for him had returned with his longing for sunlight and the warm, yellow stirring of appetite through all his being. He no longer seemed an enemy, and Nathan wondered why it had taken so long to see that. Why was it so difficult to realize that one wrestled on the ground alone? He was glad, though, that he had shown Daniels the

118

"pit" of the city, and would have liked to talk to him now about what he had seen there, but knew that was not possible for either of them.

Next morning before he took them to the airport, Nathan asked the cab driver to take a turn around town. It was a benign day, flawlessly clear and soft, perfect for the gentle little collapse into nostalgia which often afflicts the traveler. They stopped at one or two of the finer churches, and Daniels piled out with Nathan to take a farewell look. Nathan "caught" him for the last time as he stood scanning the church, feeling the texture of its walls, his hand making his whole body seem like a larger hand caressing the ancient, embedded soul of the old building. It was a perfect place for a vista of the city, though to Nathan the churches looked unusually gaunt and tired as if the sustaining spire of life within them had fallen back into the folds of itself. Below, the gloss and green of earth seemed fat with the drainage of their towers.

At the airport, when Daniels shook hands, he said with his fine smile, "Remember, Nathan, you're going to let me hear from you." Mrs. Velma gave him a kiss, and even Pennypacker managed a burlesque of the *abraço*. And then they were gone. Their plane would set down in Rio before dark and the city would claim them again as though for whatever was to happen to them there was still time.

Nathan wondered if Daniels would really answer if he wrote. The threads from one life to another were so tenuous that it was easier in the end to spin them into a cocoon. And finally you had a city to yourself that did not call you back nor send you into exile, for it was there with you wherever you went.

But he would write certainly—he was surely that sort. And Nathan would wait in the old city, listening for a voice that would call to him across space like an echo of a cry raised long ago when he had hoped that many voices, a taunting, seductive chorus, filled the woods with so many lurking friendships to which courage and desire might lead him. All that he had

119

become would be concentrated in that waiting, everything that had gone underground now exposed and drinking in this lovely air.

Behind him, as the wind stirred, there was an undulant shuddering in the leaves as if the forests of Brazil whispered through the nearest trees that he belonged to them, and the smell of the land arose with almost anesthetic richness. He had no "right" to feel, to be, to endure thus. It was simply that he did. As he looked away from the sky, down beside him at a white lily growing near the path, he saw it in enormous and breath-taking detail as under a magnifying glass which excluded all else, an ecstatic white gasp of growth where he was contained by some love which knew no bounds.

BIRD OF PARADISE

THE LONG CAR SWEPT DOWN THE AVENIDA ATLAN-
tica like a dark feather in a strong wind, and Kathleen felt
herself the only resistant burden that kept them earth-bound.
Often, when José drove her, she had the feeling of flying close
to the earth as though the sleekly projecting fenders were nubs
of wings that might slowly spread and lift her and the chauffeur,
already long before unfurled with the motion of the car, peel
them from the earth, and yield all but their shadow into air.

"Kathleen, do be back on time, at five sharp. Mr. and Mrs.
Fitzsimmons will be here for tea. He's so important to your
father at the Embassy, you know." The fretful chain of the voice
pulled all the way back to the Avenida Rui Barbosa, to the
white smile and the sudden red shadow over it as Henry Bul-
lock entered the room and came toward his wife and daughter,
twining the links of his words with those of his wife, blending
them together from long-time habit.

"Yes, Kathy, have a good swim, girl. It'll do you good. You're
looking white as a lily. But get back early. Fitz's daughter is
coming too, and your mother and I can't handle it alone. By
the way, I like that young Lieutenant of yours. Good, clean boy.
No fancy pants stuff." Towering over her, he seemed bursting
with his own sanguine strength, and, if Kathleen had felt herself showered by the fountain of his blood, she would only have
shivered like a dry flower.

Her eyes met José's in the mirror, and, as always, there was

123

the faintest suggestion of a smile on his face which lingered without development and finally slept somewhere together with fifteen years of suppressed facial expressions and the long, laconic *incommunicado* of "Yes, Miss Kathleen. Quite right, Miss Kathleen." It was at least that long, she reflected, since he had come to work for them, and she had known him longer and more constantly, though distantly, than anyone except her father and mother. It was he who had driven her to and from the American School until her graduation, and, in that atmosphere made up of swift, rootless friendships and many, many farewells, it was José who possessed a kind of vague and cloudy permanence, always there, though indistinct. The other servants in the house had seemed slight and built on hurrying feet, blown this way and that by her mother's whims and her father's rages until they had dissolved like smoke into an entirely new contingent of equally shadowy forms. But José had remained, having from the start an incisive and enduring quality even about his silence, his apparent humility before her father's rebukes, his compliance with the paternal command of never speaking Portuguese with "Miss Kathleen," and she had felt his influence as a subterranean impulse, or, as today, a nisus upward and away, never on the same level of heavy horizontality with her father and mother.

Yes, she thought, he had always been there like the shadow of her father's bright power, becoming more solid by dogged attendance, filling his insubstantiality with unobtrusive affirmations of himself as the years went by. Almost imperceptibly, he made her more strongly aware of him, though she had been trained to *see* Brazilians without taking them into account. "Kathleen, your roots are American. We'll be visitors here all our lives. Never forget that, Kathleen." She could hear her father's voice deploying itself through her time of youth, pushing ahead the years she had not earned, like an angry bulldozer in the recalcitrant soil. "Remember, Kathleen, your father does not like that Azevedo boy. They say he's got a touch of the tar brush in him. . . . Don't be difficult, darling. You know your

124

father has good ideas about such matters." Her mother's plaintive voice followed in the wake of her father like a whine of the powerful machine, and she had stumbled after the two of them with little, furtive whimpers that even to her had seemed hardly more than an exhaust of the determined family effort.

But, there, always, was José, as today in the other compartment of the car, with his restrained smile and a trace of jaunty arrogance in the way he wore his white cap and uniform over a body as compact and trim as a soldier's. So she had come to know him as a physical force by sidelong glances, the eye lifted more quickly than his—an aggregate of vital little pictures: José seen from a balcony dancing in the streets, wearing a Carnival cap like a toque of red blood, his full smile opening a quick, white wound in her stolid memory of his usual reserve: José bringing two lovebirds into the house, his lean, strong hands holding the cage of fluttering blue in almost amorous tenacity: José helping her mother from the car, supporting with perfect stance the willowy arm's uncertain pressure: José in rare dissension with her father, growing pink under his swarthy skin, as though he were being squeezed hard behind his eyes, which brimmed with a thousand filthy words held in.

Then, most endearingly, there was José at the heart of all her memories of the old days at the American School, taking her for a ride along the beach with her current favorite among the "birds of passage," as she called her classmates, speeding ruthlessly to conform with the schedule at home, or taking her time and again to the Airport through the never-ending season of good-byes, standing quietly near her with gallant detachment while she watched the plane rise and felt herself sink, seemingly each time a little lower, as though to reach a final lake of tears.

And, *now*, José at thirty-three, all gathered together during the years into the prototype of the forbidden man, to be lived with in the semi-mute world of command and compliance which buried each day more than it brought to birth until the physical continuum of their relationship was swollen with necrophiliac commitment and condonement like an old and

125

ominous graveyard. She would never understand how he had weathered the years, shifting his position noiselessly in accordance with her transformation from the girl who must be delivered and called for at school to a young lady whom he drove each day to the Embassy where she worked as a file clerk.

Since they were nearing the beach, she took out her compact and redid her make-up listlessly, working at the reflected condensation of her features as if she were tinting a miniature. The Lieutenant would expect it of her, so she would try to look her best. It was like giving someone a photograph; it might as well be a good one. That was the convenience of a certain amount of pride; it provided an easy substitute for oneself, and, in any case, there was no use starting off on the wrong foot. Everyone liked the Lieutenant and so did she; it was just that the very solidarity of the approval that surrounded him was rather fatiguing.

Glancing up with a keen sense of being watched, she saw the intent gaze of a man at a telescope in José's eyes. He looked away quickly and gave her time to recover, but the car felt unbearably close and warm as though his eyes, when they evaded her, had left the door of his hot, secret inner-vision wide open.

"You can drop me in front of the Copacabana, José," she said. He nodded, catching her attention again in the mirror, and she was thankful that his eyes were cool and sealed with disinterest.

Now that he was back in place, she wanted to smile at him, to begin somewhere to be a little less formal (after all, it had been such a long time), but the muscles hung in her face. Today would be as always, she knew—he did a perfect "disappearing act" each Sunday into that world behind his physical composite, somewhere disrobing himself in another world of nakedness than her own, and just as perfectly reappearing, precisely on time, his whole physique slightly more astringent from exercise and the sheen of his olive skin glowing after a lustral bath. Sometimes she had seen him far up the beach where he played *peteca* with a group of his dark race, clandestinely so it seemed

126

to her, and, magnifying his motion, she could see his strong, dark-downed legs sink and rise in the sand as he jockeyed for position.

When they pulled up at the curb, he opened the door expertly and helped her out, the floating motion grounded now, the car once more "the hearse," black and formal, her father's idea of dignity.

"Come back about four-thirty," she said. "Go for a swim if you like. I'll be here with Lieutenant Patterson all afternoon."

"Yes, Miss Kathleen, at four-thirty." He sounded entirely unreal to her, with the manners of an undertaker, and she hated him for his ceremonious politeness. The hot sun beat down, making her feel a little sick. The flowers around the Copacabana and even the beach had a waxy quality about them, and her brain, inflamed by the intense light, held a kind of perilous heat that threatened to liquefy whatever it impinged until she stood in pools of oily nothingness.

"Oh, by the way—" she began, and could think of nothing more. Amidst all the showiness of the landscape, there was a terrible bareness. It was as though an over-zealous property man had cleared away everything except an inarticulate feeling toward this man who would not prompt her in any way.

With her beach bag in hand, she walked down the black and white mosaic tile which simulated the motion of the waves. The familiar pattern steadied her, and the heat in her mind was ventilated as she sucked in the cool sea air. This sort of little inner drama, this suspension of packed feeling, had been growing on her, but it lifted now with the noise of her car pulling on up the street.

Lieutenant Patterson, she was sure, would be directly in front of the hotel as he had said—he was just like that—"dependable," her father would say and "predictable," as she might have added. Walking toward him through the irregular avenue of pitched umbrellas, the gilded legs, thighs, arms, so sensuously dominant that they scarcely seemed to share any significance with the shadowed faces, a heady conglomerate like fleshpots in

127

the sun, she began to worry as to what she would say to him. As always, of course, he would be informal and easy to talk with, but there was the trouble—nothing was so difficult for her as the casual conversation that Americans passed back and forth like a kind of communal meat. She had not done too badly with him so far, but she sensed that the time was near when he would be wanting the something extra which every soldier seemed to expect.

He lay very blond and tan in a circle notched on its circumference by brown arms and legs, the legend of the white god sleeping among the devoted, rising, as she approached, in a six-foot column, a sudden pressure from the languor of the ground, light on his feet as a man shot from a cannon.

What quickness and pent-up force, she thought, as she greeted him—like a loaded missile—oh, those American vitamins! He was certainly built for an air-borne world. His army haircut showed the good shape of his head, and he had a thoroughly uncluttered look in his blue eyes as though vision had been economically trained to see a few things very well. There was a little healthy red scar on his right cheek, a blemish that relieved his close-knit physical compression.

"Sorry I'm late, John. You know Papa will linger over Sunday dinner. And when Papa dawdles, it's time out for everybody." As he spread out her umbrella, dark rose like a huge overturned hibiscus, the pink suffused him with a deeper color as if the years momentarily were upon him. She had chosen this particular shade of canvas because the inward look had told her that it would heighten her ash-blonde beauty, bringing the subtle shades of the boudoir onto the beach.

"That's O. K., Kathleen," he said—she knew he wouldn't be superior or a little mad as a Brazilian might have been. "I know how your father is, just like my old man, a stickler for a good long Sunday meal. God, it can be boring, can't it? They don't seem to think you ever have anything else to do."

"Oh, I don't mind so much. I suppose I'm used to it." She

128

unzipped her cotton dress and stepped out of it, her blue bathing suit shimmering in the light. When he looked at her with pleasure, she was glad she had chosen his favorite color.

"Sure, I know how you feel." Faintly paternal, he waited for her to sit down and then stretched out on his stomach in the sand, leaning on his arms, looking up at her. "Dad really used to get me down on Sunday. I think he thought it was one day he ought to show us he was a good man."

He spoke in an easy confidential manner without the slightest notion that it represented an ellipsis, expecting her to see that father and that Sunday in Cleveland as perfectly balancing those she knew in Rio. Only the second generation in a foreign land understood that locale could become like a third parent, a seductive one, a disturber of the hearth.

"I imagine you miss your family quite a lot," she offered lamely, feeling curiously near the verge of emotions unknown to her. Perhaps this was at the root of the difficulty—the Lieutenant, just by being himself, suggested that she had been robbed of a side of her nature.

"Of course. They're pretty swell. You'd feel the same way if you knew them." He drew an outline in the sand around her feet, and, when she stirred, laughed at the bloated, grotesque doodle.

"You'd like to go back, wouldn't you?" She drew him on just to hear him include her once more in his system of reactions.

"God, yes, wouldn't you?—Oh, I forgot, you've never been there." He looked up at her and his eyes flickered with the possible need to reconsider.

"Does that matter so much? All my life I've been told what I was missing. Isn't that the same after all?" If only he could know she was really *asking,* not telling him, but his face grew confident again, and she felt accepted, but now too obtusely, as though he had just cleared up the fact that she didn't have any negro blood.

"Don't get me wrong—I have my fun. I get around anywhere

129

I am," he said, letting her last remark answer itself. "But this damn country's not my dish. Too lazy and lush for me." He tossed some sand at her legs, pelting her as though to be sure she was listening. "But I shouldn't complain. I know a lot of pretty nice people. My work keeps me busy though it annoys hell out of me too. I suppose it's a fairly routine wartime predicament. Nothing spectacular about it one way or the other—"

He drifted off pensively, but she was familiar enough with the cliché of masculinity to guess where his thoughts were. Besides she didn't really want him to start in again and tell her what he disliked about Brazil, which he most surely would unless she took his cue.

"Oh, well, with all those Wacs flitting around town you can't be too badly off," she accommodated lightly. "I notice they really clamor around the officers. It's funny to see them in their tan uniforms. Like a lot of big yellow butterflies looking for the net."

She knew she had hit him solidly "in the Services," one of the places in which he had decided not to be amused, but she couldn't resist. "You know, I see them going up and down, up and down, in the Metropole, and they all look so eager or grumpy that I've sort of divided them into 'Those with Men' and 'Those with Mission.' "

"Most of them are pretty good girls," he said. "You've got to remember some of them gave up a lot to do what they're doing. They don't always get such a good deal either. It isn't all just one happy man-hunt, you know."

How straightforward and fair he was, she thought, polite without being gallant, and, of course, there would be consideration and solicitude behind the politeness in the long run, for she could sense that he had a special niche among his orderly ideals for women where he kept his mother, sister, finally and naturally blending into "the girl." He was already appraising her and deciding whether she would fit into the mold. Thank God she was blonde, pink-cheeked, yet delicately formed, born of the concussion of a ruddy father and a fragile mother. Yes, thank God, for, after all, he was nice, very nice.

"Do you have your orders yet?" she asked, relying upon her mother's unfading American instinct (Be nice to the men, Kathleen. Let them talk about themselves. A woman listening charms, a woman talking harms) .

"Damn it, no!" He twisted in the sand as though a jolt of anger had sent a corkscrew through his body. "General Horton won't let me go. Says he needs me here in Intelligence. Fine name for my outfit, I can tell you. About all we're finding out is how many girl friends this Minister has or how many boy friends some other high monkety-monk has."

He picked up a shell and skipped it across the sand, and Kathleen had a curious longing to touch him and take the sting of his restlessness on her fingers.

"Horton really makes me sick," he continued. "He may have been a good soldier once, but he's gone entirely soft. It must have been those years in London before the War. Anyway, if there's anything I hate it's a swish general."

"Don't let the swagger stick throw you," she said, for now, perhaps as he was bound to do, he had begun to seem too thoroughly convinced about everything, and once again she could not resist a counter-tone. "Papa says he's not really a bad sort, a bit of an Anglophile, perhaps, but pretty shrewd with the military down here."

"Sure, sure, Kathleen. Your father's right in a way, but he's got to see it like that too. A business man has to play ball with that Embassy crowd. If he were my age, I bet he'd be yelling as loud as I am."

Yes, even louder, she reflected. In his "fighting years," her father had surely been one of the up-and-at-'em, do-you-want-to-live-forever school. So many attitudes belonged only to a certain time of life, so few ideals were anything but adaptations to a phase of development. Impulsively, almost with tears in her eyes, she looked at John as though she could see the silt of

131

prejudice falling into the lucid receptacle of mind and body, his skin tingeing more deeply with the national, mythic color like an outward struggling erubescence of an inward dark.

"You're right, John. Papa certainly would've seen it the way you do. No one's a better soldier than he." It was all true, of course, what he said and what she said, except that she spoke like a bad interpreter, remotely, not from consistent objectivity but from muddled loyalty and faltering belief, inspiring nevertheless such confidence that others unburdened their convictions into and through her as though she were a passage without impediment.

"This War means everybody," he continued, almost lecturing. "But it is some people *particularly,* some of us with a special sense of responsibility, maybe of guilt, I don't know, but, anyway, it means getting in there and being actually hit by the war and hitting back. And I think I'm one of those people. Do you see what I mean?"

"Yes, I think I do, John. I want to see how you feel very much, or better, *feel* how you *see,*" she added, so abruptly and earnestly that he looked up startled, and she recognized that he saw her for a moment out of character, not as just the present and outermost manifestation of images and images of "the woman."

It made her sad almost to the point of sickness to recognize an ardor she could not fully appreciate and responded to only in hectic little fevers of feeling like thrills of atavism for a land she had never seen. The War was lost in Brazil in the lavish particulars of existence; here the earth was everything and the people essentially a forest-race without self-conscious destiny. But, looking at John with his tremulous enthusiasm, she realized it would be snug to be one of the "convinced," and the small, limited world of man with its exulting intimacies seemed about to be advanced into by her for the first time.

John had been watching her intently, so unused to the type who was given to reverie. She knew he was waiting for her to go on, to say the usual things that women said to soldiers. It was

132

not his fault, of course, that she could not free him from an intellectual concept, and that, as a result, he could not quite come alive for her. All that he required was to be seen by someone like himself to have all the reality he needed.

"I can't figure you out," he said finally, flatly, with a little artificial smile to soften his frankness. "Sometimes you talk just like your father, sometimes much better, and sometimes I swear you are not listening. If you are, you don't understand anything I am saying, or, if you understand, it doesn't mean anything to you at all."

He looked exasperated, but he was really only puzzled, and she knew that his representation of the woman would save him in a moment, and that he would not try to probe deeper as a Latin might have done, resorting even to brutality to reach tears, hard-won accord, or some kind of basic response. No, his mind was already moving toward another subject. How mobile these Americans are, she thought, unaware of the impersonality of her observation.

"That's because I'm not sure," she said, picking up the train of his last remark, trying for an effect of candor which she doubted he would recognize. "All my life I've heard these things you believe in so strongly, but, you might say, at a distance. You know I look like an American, I suppose I am an American, but there's a part of me that's *bem brasileira*." She looked away so as not to seem pleading. "That's why I have to be sure."

"Oh, come on, now," he said mockingly, like a big brother ready to give her hair a pull. "You're as American as peaches and cream!"

"Look again, John. Maybe it will be a dish of *abacate com creme*," she said wryly.

"The next thing I know you'll be telling me you're not loyal. That you're some sort of spy."

"Perhaps. It would appeal to me if I could play it both ways. Then I wouldn't have to take sides. Do you see what I mean?"

"Sure. You'd like to be a Mata Hari without any of the risks, who turned out not to be a spy at all."

133

"A peacemaker, you mean?"

"Sort of. Though I wonder then if you wouldn't find that you were the only one who was left out."

He was getting restive and would go against his code in a moment and say something unpleasant, so it was better to be quiet just on the verge of disappointing him in a futile way. She couldn't help thinking that their conversation would develop into a kind of open-air forum if she continued to reply.

"Let's skip it, Kathy," he said finally, trying to look pleasantly contrite, but merely appearing boyish. "Here I've been rattling on about myself, boring you and on the point of abusing you because somehow I expected and wanted you to go along with me. A perfect case of war nerves only a few thousand miles behind the line of combat. What have I got to kick about? Nothing and everything, I suppose."

She would have liked for him to push on, for, after all, it was his intensity with its strong, aggressive rhythm pealing out his essence like a gong somewhere inside him, rather than anything he said, that really attracted her, but she knew that he had said enough, that he would suddenly remember to look at her as though she were a forgotten character in a book whose story must be developed before the collapsing arc of action could be extended.

How different the afternoon would have been with a Brazilian. With her "femaleness" as the center of interest from the start, the little drama in the sand would have turned sentimental, amatory, and dissolved itself into a mist of affection. She noticed that it was growing cooler, and there were shadows across the beach which made her think of José and wonder how all of this talk would have sounded to him if he could have overheard it.

Then John was speaking again, evenly and securely, and the regularity of his return was like the adjustment of a good machine when the hill has been climbed. "You must hear a lot of this kind of thing, a lot of gripes from some of the fellows in the Embassy who'd like to get into combat, the better sort, I

134

mean," he said, and she marveled at how unselfconsciously he had been able to mend the thread of conversation, ruptured from himself, and knit it to some imaginary point of agreement.

"Yes, a lot of the same words," she admitted, "but they don't always sound the same." She was glad she could give him a compliment, for it righted her confused sense of his value and let her see him for a moment "pure" again, as he saw himself and was probably seen by others.

"Thanks," he said, "but I suspect they are about the same. Sound and fury, you know."

But it was true—she was not trying to be kind. His "sound" was different, the words being only partly important, and she would have had to identify it to herself melodically as like a patriotic tune. Certain people *did* have sounds, like motifs running through the masses of toneless people around her. Her father was a bass drum, her mother a tinkling of glass bells, and José the rhythm of the samba, a musical watercolor full of radiance and lurking, almost phantasmal, shadows, a darkness overhung with waterfalls of light.

"What's new at the Embassy?" he asked, shifting the pivot of interest to her with his appallingly abrupt sense of timing. "I bet you're a real power around there by now. They're lucky to have someone like you who knows English and Portuguese so well. What's more you're not bad-looking." He grinned. "That must give you an 'in' with everybody."

He, too, would think of that at last. He was giving her a compliment—it was part of his system. A physical *and* a mental compliment, of course. It had all been so circular, everything they had said. There didn't seem to be any way out of it at any point.

"Oh, they've gotten used to me after three years," she said. "I was made senior file clerk last week. Gave Papa quite a bang. 'Best damn worker in the Embassy'—he went around puffing and blowing for days. You would have thought he got the promotion. . . . I'm also doing quite a lot of translating for the Ambassador now," she added, regretting how truly "small" the talk had become, quite unattached to anyone or anything.

135

It struck her as useless to begin again, to try to make him see what the Embassy was to her, like a building that had separated into a crevasse. On one side, there was the deference of the officers who accepted her as the daughter of the President of Power and Light, but who never went further than official politeness, knowing her as a "colony child" whose complete faith in them was questionable. On the other hand, there were the Brazilians among whom she might have enjoyed the role of mediator, but her mind, like a bridge continually touching and dividing, left her no centrality. He could try but he could never understand her resentment for them, their smaller salaries, the overt superiority of the officers, since he did not suspect in her the same lassitude and moral torpor which made her step-compatriots lower their eyes to the American. It would never cross his mind that she sometimes thought of herself as a kind of mulatto of the spirit with a secret *malaise* among both groups asking her allegiance.

She could sense that he was determined to spend the rest of the waning afternoon on "Sunday relaxation"—Americans had such unyielding duties toward their pleasures! They had talked about serious matters long enough, and now it was time for the workout, and she must let him go down to the water alone, remembering how burdensome American men found the non-athletic woman at such times. He would enjoy his swim better, unhampered by courtesy, and as she watched him run down to the water with incredible swiftness and agility in spite of his size—one of the mercurial race—and swim out some distance from her, she realized that that was where he belonged. Yes, he was her "golden impossibility," which no amount of physical closeness could ever make hers. You couldn't live partly underground all your life and not be hypersensitive to the light. For that was the way he affected her—like the sunlight when she got out of the car this afternoon, overpoweringly welcome at first, a kind of freedom, but finally too intense and bare, pitilessly routing all the fluttering shapes which had taken refuge in her mind.

136

Oh, in time, she could easily enough "catch" him with his obtuseness about women—that she knew. But they were on different currents, the life-flow melded of the thousands of diverse reactions of their past, perhaps a similar response to the same thing but at different times like an irremediable harmonic gaucheness. With all their possible contacts of a profound sort floating at large, they could never be "struck" with each other, possessing the same thought-feeling at any given time, and she would always feel herself a whore of longing for something he could not give her.

Suddenly, all of the crying that she had never done throbbed at the stopper of restraint as though it would wash the world away if she let it free, but with one of the supreme gestures she used on matters which others would have accomplished with the loss of no more psychic energy than is spent in raising a hand, she held on. And then, she was calm again, with the withdrawal of feeling seemingly far into the mind until the slow filling of that estuary became seductively gratifying, drawing the ominously surging power back into the body of her life like a transfusion.

When John lay down beside her again, they talked for half an hour or so about perfectly smooth and gliding subjects until she felt the conversation drifting, monotonously, hypnotically fading away as though its sound were being translated into the motion of the gulls she saw out over the water, pure and remote almost to austerity, catching, as they veered, a shaft of light like ghosts of birds tinged by the gleam of a faraway fire.

"I suppose we'd better go, John. It's nearly five," she said, and as she braced herself to rise, she turned and saw José standing not six feet away from her, his body still glistening with sweat from his game. Her first thought was one of anger (Where is his uniform?), but suddenly his nakedness seemed the only natural way she had ever seen him.

"Sorry I'm late," he blurted out. "I couldn't get out of the game till just now. I thought I'd better run down and tell you before I dressed." It was the first time he had forgotten "Miss

137

Kathleen." He spoke like a man who had known her all his life.

John rose, perplexed, waiting for an introduction which was not forthcoming, although she thought momentarily with horror that José was going to extend his hand. They stood looking at each other for an instant like a pair of impossible twins. But José quickly focused the full emphasis of his presence upon her as though he had thrown up a wall in front of the other man.

"I'll dress and get the car in a jiffy," he said, but he made no move to leave, looking down on Kathleen, the late sun streaming over him, on the curling plumes of his wind-blown head, through the hairs on the sides of his legs. As she looked up at him, her vision clouded with images of gulls, the sun seemed to permeate his body, throwing shawls of light around his arms as though to prepare them for flight, burning through his flesh with turbulent color, the dark down of his thighs like soft, sprouting feathers of gold until the wing-motion in her eyes made of him for an instant a gorgeous bird, suspended above her, poised for flight—a bird of paradise, the most beautiful thing in all the world, such as she had begged her father for long ago until it had flown out of memory, back to some deep forest of its own.

She threw a concealing hand in front of her sight, but saw from beneath its shade that José knew how intently (and how long and deeply, she feared) her eyes had rested upon him.

"Hurry!" she said, almost irritably. "I'm late for the party already." But, standing as he was on a summit, he did not step down until he had given her a time-concentrated look of scorn and contemptuous appraisal.

"Who's that joker?" John asked bluntly. "Some friend who drove you out?"

"Don't be silly," she answered with hysterical lightness. "He's my chauffeur."

"Your chauffeur?" The words sounded querulous as an oath, making it hard for her to overcome a desire to shock him.

"Of course. He's been with us for years," she said, turning

138

away just as the consternation in his face chilled the depths of her.

When the black limousine pulled up at the edge of the beach and José stepped out to open the door, he was a model of uniformed gravity. As she got in, Kathleen gave John's hand an extra pressure, which he did not return. And then the limousine was moving rapidly down the Avenida, leaving him there as vaporous as a golden mist which had momentarily escaped from a genie's bottle, and the only sensation left for Kathleen was that of wings gliding, dark wings, which could not quite clear the earth.

LETTERS FROM BRAZIL

"VIRGILIA, A WONDERFUL LETTER FROM DONOVAN!" Nancy called through the door of her bedroom. "He's asked me to come down for a visit. I think he really wants me. He sounds so enthusiastic." She laid the letter from Brazil on the breakfast tray, humping the pink drifts of the bedclothes comfortably around her.

A colored woman with an Indian cast to her features looked through the door and smiled as though skeptical of the reaction to the green, yellow, and blue airmail envelope whose contents had been read so hastily.

"That's fine, Miz Gray. Do you think you'll go?" She glanced at her mistress to see if she needed another pillow or something around her shoulders though the morning was warm and drenched with the wistaria scent of April. The breakfast hour was the matrix of the morning for them both, the one serving and the one being cared for, and something would have seemed wrong with the rhythm of life if this custom had been discarded.

"And he's been to a big Carnival ball. Everybody was there. He sounds so happy."

"I bet he was the hit of the evening. That boy always was light on his feet. Remember the last dance we gave him on his birthday?"

With the subtle confluence of mood that existed between them they looked at the photograph on the boudoir table sur-

143

rounded by pictures of the men of the family. To Nancy it had always seemed that her son was a composite of them all. Perhaps that was what the years meant, a montage of continuation and development so that all those dear faces were themselves and what would be, foreshadowing the world beyond. In that way all that had been loved and was worth loving endured. Donovan's eyes said this to her now. What a wonderful looking young man he was! Yes, with the perfectly symmetrical features, fine head and neck, the shoulders bulging against the silver frame, he was "beautiful," though there was no one she would have said that to but Virgilia.

"He says for me to come right away. He may be going to a new post, and he wants me to see Rio before he leaves," she continued as if thinking aloud.

"Flyin' down to Rio! Lordy, you'll come back doing the samba for sure. 'Scuse me, Miz Gray, I think I hear the milkman, and, if I don't get down there, Buster's gonna scare the daylights outa him barking and carrying on so."

Not wanting to be left alone, Nancy almost called after her to bring up some more coffee. When anything that required immediate action came along, she missed her husband more than ever. The letter had literally promised to knock down the walls of her house at last and open it to the south, the far South with its rich hues and shadows that inclosed such a large part of her soul. But, so many years of having most of the decisions made by someone else had taken their toll. No wonder she didn't get around much any more; it took such a long time to make up her mind.

Yet this was so unlike her, this being such a stick-in-the-mud, and she had begun to attribute it defensively to the slowing down of middle age. For, though the village-state of North Carolina was her home, she still had never wanted to be a provincial. The men in the family were the making of her, she always said—her grandfather, the Senator, who liked to quote from Goethe, "I am a Weltbürger, a citizen of the world"; her father, the distinguished judge, who had sent her abroad to

144

school; David, with whom, she laughingly told friends, she had had a "traveling fellowship" all their married life which had taken them away from Charlotte nearly every year; and then Donovan, who had gone to Rio at twenty-three to be Vice-Consul and Third Secretary of the Embassy.

As a matter of fact, until David died she could not remember having had for any great length of time a thoroughly unpacked feeling. If they had not traveled for a while, they were at least planning a trip, and that in itself put at least a part of one's thoughts in suitcases. Of course, she had loved it all, and their friends said how lucky it was that both of them had been brought up to want to travel, tutored by a concept of "Europe" which embraced a whole mythology of culture, standing for paintings and statuary and poets and princes, a rich corridor opening on an ever-widening vista of wanderlust.

But, then, after David's death, she had stayed at home, and it was only when Donovan decided to enter the Foreign Service that life seemed ready to go on as before. It relieved her in a way to think that the process of the inevitable had resumed itself, and she had encouraged her son as best she could, even concealing from him her disappointment that Rio had to be his first post. She would have preferred Paris or London or Rome, one of the cities whose every corner she knew, but, of course, with the War that was impossible.

And now she was to be given what she had wanted ever since he left, the chance to go to Rio and see for herself the part of the world whose map had been composed so perplexingly for her by the letters. She looked over toward the desk where they were stacked together in chronological order, those from her son, from Chris, and from Faith. Because of them, she didn't know whether Donovan really wanted her to come down or not. It was she, of course, who was responsible for the way they loomed like a barrier against the sky, and it was she who must cross over them now. That was what Donovan was inviting, perhaps daring, her to do.

With a sudden impulse of decision, she went to her desk and

took out the letter at the bottom of each pile. She wouldn't allow herself to dip into them at random, as she often did, for one would lead to another and she would fritter the morning away, lost in their canyon, running from echo to echo. It would give her a clean sense of architectonic to begin at the beginning again instead of wandering aimlessly through entrances and exits without any sort of clew in hand.

She looked at the envelopes, remembering what a day it had been when they arrived all together that morning two years ago with the unpredictable largesse of the wartime mails. It was easy to summon the feelings she had had at the time. Perhaps a little out of fear, she had decided to read the letter from Chris Chapin first. Bitter, sardonic, lovable old Chris! How glad she had been to learn that he was going to be Counsellor of Embassy in Rio. He had been her husband's roommate at Princeton and she had almost married him instead of David— he was so very good-looking and intelligent. Perhaps it was the little streak of bitterness in him that made her give him up—his way of seeing things "only as they were," which seemed like a kind of blindness to her.

But if he could be counted on to warn and inform her, Faith would tell her all the other things that women like to know. They had been schoolgirls at St. Mary's, they had come from the same world, and it had always been a cross to her that Faith had never married and settled down into that special corner of her life which she had reserved for her. Hers was the story of the prettiest girl in the group who somehow kept on being legendary too long, and even today, tall, graying, smart, and distinguished-looking, she had kept the unused look of beauty which had never found its proper companion. After a while, when the social world of Charlotte was embarrassingly marked off in two's and two's, she had become a clerk in the Foreign Service, working up to Ambassador's secretary, and then to the big post in Rio.

Remembering all of this, as she took the letter from Chris out of its envelope, Nancy felt that she now must read it with detachment as she sometimes reread the first chapter of a detective story just to see how the author had prepared her for the kill.

. . . Our central subject, then, is Don, for I can imagine that you will impale my letter on a voodoo knife if I fail to let you know how things are. Well, you know what he is, so we don't need to go into that. But you don't know the world he inhabits now and how he fares there. So, if I may borrow a title from a rather atrocious book by an ex-Ambassador's wife, I think I'd better tell you something about our Embassy Days—no pun intended!

First, let me start by saying that the character of an Embassy is pretty much determined by the Ambassador. Too few people at home know that, I am afraid. Much more than, say, the President, he sets the tone since after all we are a pretty concentrated group. We live in an enclave with the merits and defects of small kingdoms —competition is pitiless but the means of one's promotion lie close at hand. Consequently, the Ambassador is our Father-Image and our Temporal Deity rolled into one, and it is he who pervades our lives whether we like it or not.

Hold onto your hat while I slosh over into slang and tell you that our Ambassador is a Lulu! I think you know how anxious I was to work under him in spite of and even because of (given my demonic nature) the legends I had heard about him around the Department. He is our oldest Ambassador in point of service, and I suppose all of us want to pass through the hands of an enfabled expert at least once. I had heard that when he entered a room, he chilled the air. Well, my own veins are not exactly filled with Rosicrucian light, so I felt that I might manage the temperature well enough. But I didn't picture myself living in the middle of an Ice Age in the tropics.

To be less petty and more specific, the Ambassador (I never think of him by any other name) is an impressive looking man except that he has the uncanny effect, as you look at him, of dissolving into Pure Form, and, when he smiles, I feel a kind of Aristotelian queasiness as though an Idea winked at me from a frigid tome. He is married to a vastly rich heiress from Chicago, whom I understand he wooed and won in his fifties, and she, too, though extraordinarily stately and elegant, is rather Platonic, like the One Unchanging behind all the copies of elegant women a man might have wished he had in his bed.

We are organized intramurally according to a Cosmic Plan. There

147

is a Heaven, of course, and you know by now where that is. Surrounding Him there is a sacred ring of pretty young fellows whom I call the Cherubs. They seem to do everything from fanning their wings above His head on a hot day to carrying out the highest and lowest commands. Rumor is rife as to how low they get sometimes. Then, there is the Body Diplomatic, which includes the majority and corresponds roughly to the World and, like it, is acted upon rather than acting, and is patient, fumbling, and, we hope, endureth forever. Selah! Of course, a Heaven must have a Hell, and that's where I come in. I suppose you have gathered by now that I am not the Ambassador's Man, for I am a little too old and bony to be a Cherub. But, as Counsellor of Embassy, I am not easily mislaid though I should say my influence is largely abrasive.

Reverting to the Hierarchy, it will amuse you to know that, once in the Nether-Regions, I have found myself in the dubious role of Prince of the Fallen. When I am not drumming on my desk like a head-hunter hoping it will carry an ominous sound into the next room where the Presence resides, I find myself madly dashing and shutting the door to receive a fallen Cherub—they do fall once in a while, and seem to bruise as easily as a baby's bottom—or one of the Brave Bulls who through some misguided impulse strayed into the Pastures of Heaven. So you see I have a sort of sub-Miltonic glamor after all!

More about this later. It does sound all very phony and undemocratic, doesn't it? But don't misunderstand me, the Ambassador's diplomacy is effective as the Department would understand that word. He's been ardently cleaning the Nazis out down here like rival cutthroats; moreover he got the bases in the North as you know from the papers. And yet—I suppose I'd better sign off with just such an unfinished sentence since it better represents my state of mind.

Don't worry about Don in all this, though I thought you'd want to know what he is not so much up against as surrounded by. Like most of our young fry he has something to learn from a type like the Ambassador, and, so far, he seems to be doing all right. He hasn't made any enemies that I know of and apparently not any quick friends, which is a good thing to say about any man at this stage of the game. I hope he won't tangle with the Ambassador, for that, as I have pointed out, would be rather like falling out with God....

Nancy lit a cigarette and got up and walked around the room, finding herself even now trailed by the unpleasant aura of the

148

words just read. How like Chris she had thought the letter when she received it and what a turmoil it had put her in. It was not at all the sort of thing a father might have written about his son, and perhaps that was what she had hoped for. There had been so much she wished he could simply have told her straight for once, without his usual wit and sarcasm. It was just this side of his nature that had always made him hard to get along with. Certainly he should have realized that the last thing she wanted was a satire on the Ambassador. All that she needed to know about the man was whether he had integrity, ability, and would give her son a fair deal.

Taking up the letter from Donovan, she sat down and went on rapidly.

. . . To begin with, let me tell you how I feel about Brazil since I believe in first, fine, careless raptures. Try, if you will, to think your thought of the South to its richest conclusion, and you have Rio. Honestly, Mother, it is the loveliest part of the world I have ever seen. The Cariocas, who are immensely proud of their city, say that God was a Brazilian, and you can almost believe it after being here a few days.

I live in the newer part of the city called the Copacabana. It is a vast line of modern buildings, after Le Corbusier, strung along the beach, pale modern blues, pinks, grays, yellows, and white frothily blended—very airy and light, a mist of color-puffs and fumes like sighs and exhalations from the forest behind, and you wonder if one day they won't simply drift out to sea, having failed to become the flora that the tropics seem to demand.

You'll want to know about my living arrangements, I'm sure. My apartment is charming—three rooms, a bath, and a maid's quarters where Helena resides, a little brown bird of a girl but very bright and efficient. The apartment is not as plush as some, but, as you know, I want to live within my means and buy as many Defense Bonds as possible. It is in one of the buildings I have just described —as porous as a concrete lung, and I feel I'm always breathing air, sea, and sun, which suits a latter-day pagan very well!

Naturally how my work goes will interest you most. Suffice it to say that I have a desk but no denomination as yet. They set great store on the process of fitting in here, so I have a variety of small jobs with no predominance noticeable as yet. Sometimes I feel as if

149

I am being watched from a lot of little secret doors, even by the Ambassador, and that one day unbeknownst to me my fate will be decided upon, and I will be marked as Political, Economic, Cultural Relations, or whatever. As it is, I can best be described as floating in a diplomatic solution since it seems to be important to get the right saturation. There is something a little awesome about the Embassy, even uncanny at times, like living in an espionage story, and one often wonders what we are in league with since our major moves are apparently kept from all but a few, but I always had a yen for Whodunits, so I've never had a livelier time.

Just a few days ago we had our first staff meeting since I arrived, and the Ambassador handled it like a Czar. Most of the time he didn't say anything but sat there holding a silver letter opener at least two feet long with a crown on it and raising it up and down like a little scepter. You could see that his men had been told beforehand how to guide the discussion. It was all rather like a *grande levée,* but the funny thing is, Mother, that a good deal was accomplished, though some of the boys acted as if they had been cheated out of a bull session and were pretty mad. There's certainly a lot of razzle-dazzle about it all, and I'll have to be here a good while longer before I put it all together.

On weekends I spend a good deal of time on the beach so I'm very tan and fit. The hangout for the Embassy is Arpoador where the Ambassador holds court under a huge umbrella with Colligan, Scott, and Davies, three of the younger men, while all the rest are spread out under lesser canvases at a discreet distance from the imperial tent, and there is something a little nomadic about it, even forlorn, in spite of the exquisite setting. Colligan and his pals are the butt for a lot of coarse talk, but I prefer to chalk it up to envy and gossip which naturally is a favorite pastime of Americans abroad. Anyway, I haven't been invited in under the umbrella and doubt if I should want to.

So far I'm getting along famously with the Brazilians. You remember the letter of introduction Mrs. Bennett gave me to the Medeiros family. Well, they've been awfully good to me. And they have a daughter, Amalita, who is a real dreamboat! She gave a party for me last week—I don't know how she found out it was my birthday —and invited more goodlooking girls than you could shake a stick at. American men seem to be in great demand down here. I never had it so good at home!

But don't think I'll go off the deep end. I haven't forgotten our many talks, and I've thought a lot about them. Remember you once said that I should carry the message of myself abroad. Well, that phrase stuck with me because at the time I felt pretty sure what it meant. But, honestly, now I'm not so sure, and I think I will learn that only here. At home we are so much a part of a certain background that we tend to merge into it. Here we stand out in relief, and it's rather startling at first, but, in the long run, it should indicate a number of things more clearly. I hope this makes sense to you. Anyway, I think you know I want to be a good officer, and if I should take a tumble, I'll do my best to land on a cushion.

I see Uncle Chris and Aunt Faith every day, and they've been extremely helpful. With such a contingent from Carolina, I don't see how things could go wrong, do you? . . .

No matter how often I read it, it doesn't sound any different, she thought as she put the letter back in the envelope, laying it under a book as if to silence it. It was a fine letter, really, the good, long one she had wanted. Donovan's voice was there, the tone was all right in that way. But he had forgotten to tell so many things she had hoped to hear. Perhaps, after all, she had wanted most to know that he was the same, that the new life hadn't made such an abysmal difference. The disappointing thing had been that it was there, the beginning of a change. More than anything else, this gave her a feeling of how far Rio was from Charlotte.

She was a little ashamed to be rereading the old letters at all when the new one required her attention. David always said it was the Scarlett O'Hara in her that allowed her to think of whatever suited her at the time. But to stop now would be rather like refusing to listen to the other side of the question, she thought, as she picked up the letter from Faith.

. . . I won't tell Donovan but I don't mind telling you that the Ambassador has been quite impressed with him and that things ought to go very well if he keeps his head. And, my dear, he could not be associated with a more wonderful man! As you know, I've been with several other Ambassadors, but this man is a model for them all. You've seen him in the news, but none of his pictures do him justice. He's over six feet with an absolutely fascinating way of carrying himself, and though nearly sixty, looks ten years younger.

151

And, my dear, he has the most magnificent head I've seen on any man, with a wonderful widow's peak coming down to a splendid forehead, blue eyes that look at you seldom but drench and drown you in their comprehension when they do, a good masculine mouth, and a chin that draws its power all the way down from the arches of his brow. I can hardly keep my eyes off him when I'm taking dictation! Besides, I've never known anyone so easy to work for. He knows exactly what he wants to do and does it without any fuss or waste motion, though his responsibilities are terrific.

The hue and cry among some, of course, is that he is un-American, undemocratic, and this just makes my blood boil. Which brings up the subject of gossip around the Embassy and reminds me that I'd better scotch the whole thing with you since some of it may work its way back and give you some sleepless nights. The things they say about the Ambassador! He's ruthless, inefficient, a snob, a dandy, he comes from a defunct Southern family, respects only people with money, is a Nazi (sic!), he's mentally cracking up, and so on and so on—the Song of the Malcontents, I call it.

Worst of all they make a great scandal of the fact that he takes an interest in the younger men in the Embassy. I happen to know there is absolutely nothing wrong there. He likes young people, and they relax him from such an intense schedule. He has a great sense of handing on the traditions of the Service, and naturally it's the young men whom he can teach. If you knew some of the old fogies he has around him, you would understand why he looks to the young. Even Chris Chapin, I'm sorry to say, has fallen in with this group, and he and I have had some hot arguments. Anyway, you don't need to worry about it for Donovan's sake who, even if it were true, obviously wouldn't be involved.

Rio, my dear, is simply enchanting. Everyone raves about the city and landscape which are incomparably beautiful, of course, but it's the people I adore. I don't think you can find a more socially graceful sort than the Brazilians. Particularly the men, who really know how to treat a lady as the girl at the glove counter would say. Honestly, they make you feel they are casting rose petals over you. And the women are charming, too. You should see them at parties in their stunning and original hats, moving around as though they had never bumped or crashed into a thing in their lives. Really they seem to have a secret elastic in their gestures. I suppose if I had to use a word for their effect upon you, it would be *floral.* They don't know what it is to be self-conscious, and being with them is rather like listening to the sound a flower or leaf would make if it

152

could talk—so beautifully natural, and yet you know they must have practiced their lives before a mirror.

Naturally I see Chris quite often in spite of our differences and, as you can imagine, the tropics haven't done a thing for him. These bright skies, I'm afraid, rather clash with his temperament. But I suppose it's good to have at least one troubled conscience around, and, of course, he's a dear after all and will surely be ready with the ice pack if one lives too gaudily. . . .

Nancy put down the last page with a perverse satisfaction. No, she hadn't been mistaken about any of the letters. They were bewildering in emphasis and for her purposes all wrong. She had expected a triumvirate of voices telling her about Donovan, a little collection of confidential reports. But the perspective was reversed, and the three of them lurked in the background as pathetic as children peeping out of the woods in a strange, lush, tropical land where the Ambassador loomed like a mythical giant. It seemed to be an odd way of talking about her son. What oblique letters, all of them, after all! She had pictured the Ambassador as a rather large figure, yes, but in the far backdrop of their lives, almost as though painted on the scenery rather than animating it. But there were three pairs of eyes that followed him like concealed spotlights on the hero-villain. It had been disturbing, roundabout; it threatened to admit into her life a powerful stranger who hinted at blackmail of established memories.

After that, the house in Charlotte had never been the same, for the letters from Brazil blew into it like deciduous leaves, an atonement from a tropic world that knew no autumn falling, and often she felt as though she could barely move among the drifts of their presence. Sometimes, as she looked at them on her desk, they threatened to hiss, rise up in a coil like a blanched serpent and sting her, and then again when she strung them together in another light they seemed harmless as a flamboyant bracelet which meant nothing but its variety. At least there was no doubt, as she told Virgilia, that Donovan, Chris, and Faith had blown hot, cold, damp, and dry, and indeed sent her a

153

world of weather from a land that was supposed to be one of eternal sunshine.

As the War wore on, the letters had seldom come in pairs, almost never in trio, so, at least, the chameleon changes of mood were spaced a day, a week, a month apart, as the case might be. But try as she might she couldn't help getting upset if she heard from Chris in a specially cynical mood. In spite of herself she had been affected by his version, his propaganda line, as she sometimes thought of it. It could turn itself on, particularly at night, like a radio hidden in the wall, only perhaps to be mercifully drowned out by some delicious strain of Faith's transports over Rio. But at least Chris and Faith were more or less dependable. It was Donovan who led her one way and then another until she often felt she could not stand his variability any longer. The thought of the way those streaks of sound had laminated her sleep for so long recalled forcibly how her life had been transformed by and depended upon the letters. Indeed her entire mentality had become like a gong which the postman's coming could make quiver with mingling reverberations for days after.

Now, the letter from Donovan which had just arrived must be reread or the point of having looked at the others would be lost. But she didn't feel up to it. Slipping on her robe, she decided to go downstairs for a while and perhaps take a stroll around the garden. She had always loved her home in spite of a footloose longing for travel, and one of the most painful things about all this business in Rio was that it had somehow unsettled the familiar dedications. Her devotion required her son's as well, and a frightening aspect of his letters was how little they referred to anything they had in common. After all, she sometimes wondered, was she beginning to receive letters from a stranger? Today she must make up her mind whether she was to go and find out for herself. Of course, she could plead short notice and ask for more time to make plans, but what was the point in putting off a matter about which she had brooded for so long?

When she went outdoors, the blaze of the southern spring

154

that had flickered gently through the bedroom hit her full force. The banks of forsythia were swollen with yellow, and all the flowering shrubs were humped high with bloom as though some rich breath had inflated them. It was beautiful and at the same time tiring since she had to swim in its opulence all alone. Everywhere she turned reminded her of Donovan for they had often worked in the garden together. Taking several turns around the flower beds she noticed how rank and full of weeds they looked now that she took care of them herself. It was no use; she might as well go back in, read the letter, and settle down to some sort of decision.

She picked a bunch of jonquils and, leaving them in the hall for Virgilia to arrange, went upstairs. Since the letter still lay on her night table, she decided to get back into bed. There was no need to read the first part; the travel plans would only deflect her from all the rest again.

... Before I tell you about Carnival though, I'd like to clear up one or two things which I gather from your letters have been worrying you for quite a long time and which should be straightened out I think before you come down. Pardon me for saying so, but I detect the hand of Uncle Chris in all of this. If you've been taking his version of things down here too seriously, I'm surprised you haven't phoned the State Department and demanded that they send me home by Air Express, thoroughly disinfected of tropic vice before crating, of course. The trouble with Uncle Chris is that he is such a *literalist*. The Ambassador sweeps up in his Cadillac with chauffeur and footman and that can mean only another example of the old so-and-so's arrogance, whereas it may be that the Ambassador understands the Latin love of display so well that he knows it is expected of him.

The fact is, Mother, that Uncle Chris should never have been a diplomat. He is too incorrigibly American, too local, though he thinks he is none of these things, and I suspect that is why he has never been given a higher post. Which brings up *my* opinion of the Ambassador, and I know you have waited an unconscionably long time for it. Let me say frankly that I both admire him and am disturbed by him, though not for the same reasons as Uncle Chris. I don't mind telling you that for a long while I studied him as a

155

model because I wanted to know what makes a successful Ambassador, but I have known how, I trust, to keep my distance when necessary, and he has respected this at all times. He once said to me, I'm not looking for disciples, Mr. Gray, but students. I knew then he didn't mind my using him as a pattern, that it was actually a relief that someone had recognized to what lengths he has gone to establish the form of his life.

You may object that he is living in an act, a pose, which, of course, is true, but he has done so because he thought it was necessary to the conditions of his profession. While Uncle Chris would picture him to you as a rather cliché Prince of Darkness, I think of him as a supreme Aesthete of Diplomacy, a man with a positive passion for making things work, for bringing them off without a slip-up of any kind. Of course one of the dangers of such love of perfection is that it can tend to make a man somewhat ruthless as the years go by and human thoughtlessness keeps endangering the structure of the dream he has lived by. I suppose this is one of the ironies of perfectibility. Was it Nietzsche who said that in order for something to be born, it has to be loved more than it deserves to be loved? I think there is no doubt that the Ambassador has erred in this way.

I am convinced he knows this, and that is what I meant when I said I found him disturbing. He is not, I believe, nearly so sure of himself now that he has arrived as he was ten years ago when he was still on his way up. Though Uncle Chris would literally swallow his uppers, as Virgilia says, to know I was writing this, the thing that worries me most about the Ambassador is a real lack of confidence. This, perhaps, partly explains his affection for the young who have not yet had to learn what it costs to build such a life.

Try to understand the Ambassador's position in the following way, Mother. On the one hand he is committed to spreading the influence of the United States abroad but only in so far as it expedites world unity and harmony, or so the theory of our government goes. To do this he has frequently had to employ aristocratic means since that is often the only comprehensible and feasible way in the older parts of the world, and, of course, to be entirely honest, the method has suited his temperament.

He has pursued his course all these years, I'm sure, in the belief that the qualitarian like himself could exist in some vague undetermined way in such a society. Operating under this belief he has gone on to achieve great mechanical grasp of international relations and to ride out the tremors of an age in transition. But all the

156

while through the clouds of the national dream he has been near-ing the actual fact of a world dedicated to a classless society, and it is no longer so probable that there would be a place for his type of man in such an order. In other words, he has been helping to ensure the death of the only kind of society which had a secure place for him.

Though none of this, of course, is immediate, the Ambassador suffers from the fear of being engulfed in One World, the logical conclusion of the democratic faith. If it works, apparently the death of qualitarian individualism will ensue; if it does not, America will have to draw in the swirling cape of brotherhood and welfare and admit defeat—the outlook either way makes for shaky nerves. You can see, then, that it would be no fun at all to be the Ambassador. Out where he is looking, there is nothing but the pitiless abstraction of the Future.

I think I realized last night after the Embassy Ball more clearly than ever before the Ambassador's loneliness and aloneness. It was nearly dawn, the last guest had just left, his wife had gone to her room, and the Ambassador had let the last of the servants go to their quarters some time before. He asked me to stay on a moment and help him with the final shutting up of the house. It had been a tremendous evening; the ball was a magnificent success, but the Ambassador was utterly exhausted. I could tell that from the lines in his face though he was still his usual model of sustained com-posure. He had worked terrifically hard all evening—I had watched him from time to time, making the rounds, dancing with as many as possible, both Brazilian and American. It was easy to spot him in the crowd as he was the only one who was unmasked and not in costume. As you can imagine, he stood out powerfully as though his evening clothes were the only costume there, a kind of basic one he found he could not yield. Being so tall, he towered well above the swirling, turning mass of color which almost seemed to gravitate around him.

As we went silently from room to room putting out lights, I felt positively eerie. You know how appallingly empty a big house can be after an enormous number of people have been there—as though it had suffered an arterial drainage. The fact that the Embassy is full of white marble and a kind of impersonal, applied grandeur everywhere you look didn't help either. I had the feeling, as we tried the windows, that we were walking around in a vast tomb, as much trying to get out as to keep anyone from trying to get in.

157

When we got back to the foyer, he turned to me with a tired smile and said, "Well, Mr. Gray, you're the last one, I see. It was quite a celebration, wasn't it? Thanks a great deal for the help in closing up. I trust you won't have any trouble in getting home."

Well, Mother, this is hard to understand, but a terrible feeling swept over me. I felt like a deserter, or, as though there were some mysterious situation involved in which only one of us could escape and he had picked me. I'll never forget how he looked then, waiting there in the dim morning light, a few streamers still clinging to his evening clothes. He reminded me of a denuded axis, a pole of the carousel left standing alone. It made me understand better than ever before what a bare and ultimately unadorned thing strength is.

After reading the above, you won't be too surprised, then, to know I've made an important decision. It is definitely expected that the Ambassador will be sent to a European post, probably Paris, as soon as our Embassies are reopened there. He has already let me know there'll be a place for me if I want it. I've never given him a direct answer, because I've been undecided for a number of reasons. But I wonder now if many of them were not selfish, even fearful, ones. Of course, I could always stay here, which would certainly be easier and more comfortable, but if the opportunity of the new post comes along, I don't see how I can turn my back on it. All of this probably sounds much too tall, hortatory, and stuck-up, and I won't mind if you simplify it for yourself and say, "Donovan, God bless him, just wants to go to Paris."

At any rate, there is all the more reason for you to come down as soon as possible. As I said, it'll not only be a grand trip for you and a joy to me but it'll give you a chance to see for yourself how things are down here. Let me know right away when to expect you.

Aunt Faith continues to be a darling, and Uncle Chris, as I have pointed out earlier, continues too. So all is well.

So all is well. That was the phrase to hang onto, desperately, if need be. Nancy knew it, forced its admission upon herself, as she laid the letter on top of the others. Slipping downstairs again, careful not to arouse Virgilia, she began to prowl around in her own house, wandering from room to room. There was no doubt about it, not counting Virgilia who was almost a primitive phase of her own personality, no one lived there any more but herself. Herself and the sound of those damned invasive letters! But how ridiculous! It really wasn't all of them, it was

158

one, not Chris or Faith, but Donovan alone who had been trying all these months to get through to her. In that respect, it
was rather like the old days when she was entertaining guests
and he used to repeat his question or statement through the
medley of conversation, not rudely but just patiently, until
everyone suddenly paused and listened to Mrs. Gray's bright
little boy.

But that was where the Ambassador came in too. That terrible, that awesome man! Donovan had spoken of abstractions.
Well, all these months she had been walking around and around
one where she feared he was imprisoned, where she hoped he
was free. An abstraction, yes, but only so at its core, for there
before it were the Ambassador and her son meeting, touching,
passing, with some secret cloth of knowledge in their hands, and
it was impossible to tell whether they wound or unwound anything at all or merely made a mysterious, weaving motion
around an emptiness.

Yet, now that she was free to see everything for herself, she
didn't want to go. She might as well admit it today as tomorrow.
Even the thought of all the preparations she would have to make
unnerved and fatigued her, and she had to recognize that without knowing it she had been at heart a stay-at-home all along.
She would have to write Donovan in the afternoon and tell him
something tactful—health, business affairs, any one of the reasons that everyone had to accept.

But the decision oppressed her, and the house seemed as
suffocating as the bed. She would have liked to rush out onto
the lawn, but there was the garden wall, then the edge of town,
and so on. There would never be an end to it, and she would
have to turn back and admit she had never found her limits
and was not so sure she wanted to though Donovan was out
there somewhere. She couldn't stop him now, not even with a
desperate wave of the hand. He wouldn't turn back. And there
was nothing left for her but her home, her town, her state, lifted
high in loneliness like a widow's walk where she who let the
beloved go waits for his return.

THE EDGE
OF THE FOUNTAIN

On the terrace of the Bolero, Dr. Edwin Woodley sat looking out over the Copacabana beach, sipping a *cafézinho*. He did this often now after his afternoon class at the University of Brazil since it gave him back that largesse of soul which he had preserved as carefully as he could through forty-five years.

One could tell at a glance that he was a person of culture and intelligence. His baldness merely served to increase an imposing intellectuality as though incessant thought had cleared away the tangle and growth of hair in order that the bone structure might shine through more powerfully, and his skin, though of a pink and pleasing good health, showed no trace of jowls. It was a countenance reminiscent in over-all impression, though the detail was different, of the shorn power, the denuded grace, the handsome, glowing mentality which appear in some of the photographs of Henry James, on whom, so it happened, Dr. Woodley was an authority.

This was the fourth week of eight which he was spending in Rio on leave from his professorship at Northwestern to teach a seminar group and deliver some public lectures on Hawthorne, Melville, Poe, Whitman, Dickinson, James, and the other "greats" of American literature. He was there on invitation from the Brazilian Government, the sort of "guest" which our State Department underwrites, allowing the entertaining country to save face by paying a token part of the expense involved.

163

As it happened, however, Dr. Woodley had been having an extremely difficult time extracting even this small gesture of the University's faith in him. Consequently he had been forced to go from one to the other to see about the matter, each man seeming to be an office without an occupation, until it had all come to be a little sinister, like an anecdote from a Kafka story, as though there were a monstrous tyrant behind all the rooms of officialdom to which he must pay some particularly degrading tribute before he could receive his due.

Matters were not helped at all by the fact that the Director of the Faculty of Philosophy, his immediate sponsor, was visible but non-accessible. He was a fat white worm of a man with sorrowful black eyes, but apparently someone to be reckoned with, a clever master of political maneuver who never got up until twelve o'clock in order to catch the world at the height of things. It was he who started the process of passing Dr. Woodley from hand to hand as though the incorruptible American might be worn down into some amenable shape of moral fatigue and capitulation.

Moreover, neither the University nor the Embassy, which took a dim view of professors and esthetes scurrying around in time of war, had provided any publicity for the public lectures, and, though these were brilliant, quite the best that any American had brought there, Dr. Woodley found himself faced by a rapidly dwindling audience dropping like beads from a broken string until there was the mortifying experience of catching oneself "counting the house" as though in some evil sort of way the number of heads present was to signify the right of survival, the whole business becoming finally a kind of spiritual Inquisition.

These strata of the "situation" in Rio streaked Dr. Woodley's mood as he looked out over the water, letting the gulls draw the delicate strands of his loneliness to some indeterminate point. He was neither Embassy, nor Colony, nor the professional man with a demonstrable and practical defense of his presence, the engineer, the sanitation man, the "expert" of one kind or

164

another. Nor, of course, could he align himself with the most powerful group of all, the businessmen who had swarmed into Rio on the waves of the War, making deals on the one hand, preaching democracy on the other, each one like a taut rope of the American way, stretching the material of the Idea to include everyone like a sort of mythic parachute that would save the world. Such an intellectual coverall Dr. Woodley detested, and he had refused to dangle in the big balloon of misrepresentation and nonsense with all the rest.

It was curious in a way that he should be in Rio at all—he admitted that to himself freely—recognizing the mixture of motives not altogether fitting into a single pattern. The decision to come to Brazil was one of his freer, more impulsive, basic moves—perhaps an unconscious answer to the chaos of the war, impelled by the notion that order and the sense of beauty as well should be tested in such a time. Perhaps, also unconsciously, he had a "southern exposure" in his soul, brought up, as he had been, in the cold country of Minnesota, and there was an unrecognized longing to warm himself in a more ardent and beguiling climate. Possibly the lure of Rio, a word blent of dazzling beaches, dark folk, the moistures and fecundities of desire, had stirred in him the slumbering wish to wear the many-colored robe of abandon.

His reflections as he finished his *cafézinho* and called for another had become more agreeable. Yes, thank God, he told himself, life and discipline had done that much for him. He knew how to dismiss the unpleasant as well as to force himself to return to it. And, in spite of the Ministry's anonymous bewilderments, the Embassy's indifference, he was determined to find the Brazilian experience rewarding—he would enjoy himself and get his work done. He would "possess" Rio, its startling crudities and unexpected beauties, mainly, as he had observed, transplantings from Europe, the old garden of the imagination to which he had been for so many summers a "passionate pilgrim." And he would observe the people, get to know them whenever possible, learn some snatches of their language, and

165

become an *aficionado* of the best that was in them. All that mattered, as Ezra Pound had said, was "the quality of the affection."

As this caressive mood spread gently around him, he turned, looked out beyond the crowd again, over the crushed white of the surf, to the far emptiness of the ocean's sweep, assuaging himself with its containment. But, abruptly, he was brought back for there had been a thump nearby like the sound of a heavy fruit falling on stone.

A woman had sat down clumsily in the chair on the other side of the wicker table. She was not one of those Dr. Woodley had been resting his eyes on, the lovely Carioca girls who were like sticks of perfume on a simmering fire of pleasure, but looked indeed as though she had been cast down in anger, a lump of humanity, seeming all the more fleshly solid from having struck the sides of the world too often before arriving at what was apparently the bottom but which might yet give way into lower stories of disaster.

"*Monsieur*," she said, shifting heavily from her crumpled position, her whole body bulging from the chair like a final belching sigh. "I want to talk to you." She leaned forward in a conspiratorial hunch. "You will give me a few moments of your time, no?" It was curious that she combined French address and English discourse, the latter spoken with the intonation and accent of some *école* of long ago, giving Dr. Woodley the impression that she had mistaken his identity.

"Pardon me, *Madame*," he said, rising hastily, aware that his neatness, his modest blue suit, presented an unusual contrast to her dishabille, creating the tension of two worlds in the little café. "I'm sorry. Perhaps I have taken your table."

"No, no, no, *Monsieur*," she said with unexpected violence. "Sit down, please. I want to talk with you. You are an American, no? Then you can help me." The inert mask strained for a smile as though the lips were loaded with stone.

"What is it that I can do for you, *Madame*?" he asked as he sat down slowly. "I'm afraid I don't understand." But the signal

166

of "handout" flashed ahead and he began to feel wary, fumbling at the same time toward his pocket.

Another careful look at the woman convinced him of his first impression. She was unmistakably European, naturally a refugee, one of the lonely and forlorn horde which he had seen in the streets. Over her wisps of sandy gray hair, she wore an old blue sun-scorched tam which gave her an even more squashed and dumpy look at the same time that it seemed to have shorn her of the halo of civilization which beautifully coifed hair gives to women. It was the head-covering, even the helmet, of necessity, the downward fall. Her woolen trench coat bore no relation to the weather, for the afternoon was warm. Apparently it was worn constantly, even slept in like the pelt of an animal—a rumpled, dismal affair of dingy tan, smudged with tawny beach sand of some abandoned siesta or evening sleep of a demoralized sense of locality. There was a brooch of red and white crystal at the neckline, rather chic in its time perhaps, but an horrendous gewgaw now, a gaudy pustule of life's deceit. There were also visible between the lapels of the coat and below its border the remnant of a silk dress like a tattered flag of her *ancien régime.* Beneath, the bony poles of bare legs, burnt black as mummy flesh by the sun, pushed down into the filthy swaddling of a pair of old sneakers.

Out of this packed imagery of degeneration, the face loomed somewhat, but not greatly, startling in its sense of life not all yet hammered back into the animal pulp. This was most frightening of all to Dr. Woodley, the flicker, the spasm of humanity, which was worse than death, like the twitch of an insect jolting the mind into a last minute appraisal and regret for that snapping at one point in its network of the basic thread which unites all living things.

"You must help me, *Monsieur,*" she said. "I have been wronged, horribly mistreated. They have beat me, they have put me in jail. They are pigs, these *brasileiros,* filthy pigs! Look at me, *Monsieur.* I am a woman of class, I am a graduate of the Sorbonne. But look at me. See what they have done!" The face

167

puckered up in a grimace of tears which would not flow, but the effect, summoning more strength of passion than could be spared, had the force of a phantom-geyser. "But you, *Monsieur.* You have a good face. You will help me, yes?"

"But—but, *Madame.* I do not know you," Dr. Woodley said with reluctance, feeling curiously ashamed a moment after. "I'm afraid I don't know what your trouble is."

"But you will help. You can help me. You are an American!" The last word she flung at him like a dash of some final stimulant as she watched the closing expression of doubt, mistrust, and bewilderment. And then the walls of communication, throttled so long, rose in a shrill babel of French, English, German, Portuguese, as though the fusion of all language, rising and gorging the disused tube of the throat, were necessary to lift the mighty wail of her heart.

The rushing spout of words attracted a white-coated waiter who, evidently familiar with the woman, started to usher her out. She cringed at the sight of him, refocused her face and gave him a withering look that died of its own extravagance. Dr. Woodley waved the man away vigorously, maintaining his grip on an impulse which might have taken just such an opening of escape as had been offered it.

"Go ahead, *Madame.* I'm listening. I assure you no one will disturb us," he said, but the very connivance which he thereby cast around the unknown, this at least provisional acceptance without possessing the facts, was disturbing, for it put him in league with the chimaeras of destiny.

"Oh, *Monsieur,* thank you, thank you. You are not like the others. I have found a true American at last," she sighed, and laid on the table a greasy handbag, stuffed out of all proportion like a peasant's sack, a swollen tumor of her wanderings.

Then the story came out in ejaculations, rivulets, sudden passionate torrents of accusation and limp stretches of self-pity —disconnected, rambling, splenetic, febrile. It aroused a strangely glimmering feeling of the havoc from which all ideas must once have raised themselves. The words rose free, rational, and

168

shining, cleansed of the entangling muck for a moment, and then sank back to the diffusion and defeat of their struggle.

But, in spite of the thrashings of her distress, the fragments of a past emerged. It appeared that she was not French but Yugoslavian, having come to Paris with her daughter after the death of her husband many years before. With income from work she obtained there, they had lived happily, using their free time to take courses at the Sorbonne, discovering all sorts of hidden affinities with the French, content to be expatriates forever. But the War had thrown them into a panic, and they had escaped to Lisbon just before the fall of Paris. There they had waited on the ominous threshhold, pondering the possibilities endlessly, finally deciding on separate explorations into the immediate future, a division calculated to avoid a single catastrophic defeat. The daughter, a successful photographer in Paris, was to go to New York, being perhaps more able to buck the bewildering enormity of the city, whereas she was to seek the more genial climate of the south, and the one who fared better would send for the other in a final healing of sundered forces.

As it turned out, there had been nothing in Rio for her. The city appalled her as blatantly primitive or superficially civilized, a jungle travesty of Europe. Unlike many of the refugees who had scurried under the cynical protection of *gran finos,* she could not pay lip service and had gone down, down, making, as it were, an excavation into ultimate possibilities of misery until her life had become a temporary footing in darkness down which the aimless hand was lured to throw a stone.

Her daughter had done better, though her position too was extremely precarious, and it was a question, not yet resolved, as to whether she should let go of the slender rope from which she dangled, go to Brazil and get her mother, only perhaps to flounder with her in a final embrace of defeat, or stay in New York and hold on with all her might until some feasible way of reunion could be worked out.

"All that I want, *Monsieur,* is just a visa," she said finally, and the last word fell from her mouth like a jewel hoarded

169

there. "I have talked and talked with your Consul. And now they will not let me see him. I have not enough money, he says. I tell him that I have a lovely, kind daughter who will take care of me. But, no, no, he says. There would not be enough. She cannot guarantee my support, and I would only make her starve. I weep and cry, and he tells me the truth. There's a matter of your record with the police, *Madame,* he says. They have told him I am crazy. Twice I have been in jail already because I do not like the Government here, because I want to go to America. And they beat me and tell me I am crazy."

"Well, *Madame,* I am very sorry to hear this. If you think I can help, I'll see the Consul tomorrow," Dr. Woodley said, for he could not deny this woman. Everything he believed in told him he should not. "Perhaps he'll listen to me. Perhaps—"

"Oh, thank you, thank you, *Monsieur,*" she broke in. "You will do it for me. You will get me the visa!"

And then her speech went to pieces altogether, mingling past, present, premonitions of the future, dashed against each other in negating phrases. Dr. Woodley did not know what to think. He wanted to feel for her, to take her side. But perhaps she was mad after all. It was getting late, and he excused himself, leaving her babbling and burbling like an old cauldron of despair and vengeance.

Standing in the bus line tumid with the crowds of a war society, he was astonished to see that the "woman" had added herself, a grimy, dessicated segment, to the fat caterpillar of people strung out along the walk. Well, she, too, must be going somewhere, but the whole thing had begun to give him a sticky, crawling feeling, and he longed for his bath and dinner. As though waiting for a receptive mood, the voice of one of the "authorities" with which his mind was stored, Santayana, the old philosopher among the Blue Nuns of Rome, quite unexpectedly drifted into recall: "It is possible to love human beings only in solitude." But he rejected it promptly, as he had always done, contesting the Olympian aloofness of such detachment.

170

Once ensconced in a seat buttressed by a rather gross Brazilian, he glanced behind him occasionally and saw her, still muttering away, waving, smiling, then looking at him blankly, while the gray bus lurched along frantically. As he got out at the Hotel with relief, he remembered that she had forgotten the most important thing of all. She had never given him her name! All that run-on talk and not the final words that say "I am."

When he had bathed, and dined in the lovely *salon* of the Gloria, now a place of enchantment, a turret of pleasure on an angry hill, he felt much better, letting the plumes of his feelings shake out their radiance again with that focus on the agreeable and beautiful, as long as circumstances permitted, which more than once had "saved" his life. Remembering that he was going to hear Jennie Tourel in a concert of French songs at the Teatro Municipal, he descended to the *portaria* briskly. But as he hailed a taxi, the woman emerged from the shadows beyond the columns like a taunting denial of his well-being. This was ridiculous, absurd! He was not to be haunted. But he held on to himself, remembered his wish to be kind, and spoke pleasantly. Driving away, he looked back furtively as though wings of pursuit might unfold from within her, but she had leaned on the bulging belly of the lower wall, a wizened child against a heavy mother.

But it was not until he returned from the theatre and found her still leaning against the mottled yellow façade, her tan-brown dinginess like a protective coloring, that he got some inkling of what he was in for. This was too much! He had hoped to slip in unnoticed, but stirring from her stupor as though a secret mechanism had awakened her, she came weaving through the shadows, losing him just as he gained the revolving doors. The little thrill of escape took him back to his childhood. It was like Halloween. He was being chased by a witch!

But as he got into bed, he remembered her with overwhelming pity. He should not have run from her, he would do what he could for her tomorrow. He wanted and needed to sleep after

171

an exhausting day in the maze of the University, but his famous power of concentration had finally deserted him. The voice of Tourel was still ringing softly in his ears, richly evocative of the old days, Paris of the "then," Paris of inviolable beauty, and he could have let himself float down to sleep in the flow of these memories, but they were constantly crossed and deflected by the muddy current of the woman's life, and it seemed that a thrombus moved in the stream of all things beautiful.

The next morning he went in early to see the Consul, a tall, big-boned man with an air of casual strength, who listened to him professionally, yawned a little as from a story heard too often, saying finally, "Yes, Professor Woodley, you needn't worry about not knowing the name. I know who she is. It's an old case. Been running on for several years. Dona Carlota, the kids in the street call her, though that's not her right name. They've even made up a samba about her, I understand. Quite a character around town. It's been one long headache to me. The old lady simply won't listen to reason, won't get it through her head that we can't grant her a visa under present circumstances."

The Consul raised his hand slightly, requesting the indulgence of silence as Dr. Woodley tried to interrupt him.

"You see, Professor," he went on, "there's simply no legal way of doing it. She has no money here or in the United States. I understand she lives on a pittance sent down by her daughter. Then there's the problem of her mental condition. The Brazilian authorities have declared her unbalanced, and this disqualifies any prospective entrant to the United States. It's a pity, of course, but, Professor, if you want my opinion, I think the police are right. The old lady is bats, simply bats. It was good of you to come in, but, if I were you, I'm afraid I'd just forget about it." He turned away from his visitor and glanced through the window across the bay, lazily dropping the subject into the vat of blue, dissolvent color.

172

Dr. Woodley was stunned and angry when the Consul stood without shaking hands, surgically detached like a man in charge of a corrupt program of euthanasia. But there were classes to be met; one's emotions must be buckled in. The day beckoned to him out of its cloudless beauty, and he must trust it again, he told himself, as he walked toward the University under an avenue of palms whose swirling fronds had nothing but ease and forgetfulness in their rustling luxuriance. And yet he knew very well what probably lay ahead. One of the professors would stop him in the hall and tell him the story of an intrigue or persecution among the faculty, perhaps compare his salary with the prevailing standard as a suggestion of encroachment. To his colleagues he had become a sort of magic lantern into which they could insert "slides" of the intramural struggle against the Ministry of Education. Often he was prepared to commit himself, when the contradictory view was convincingly inserted into the other side of his thinking by another colleague.

Late that afternoon, as he left the Faculty of Philosophy, having been spared the conspiratorial tête à tête for once, he was confronted by Dona Carlota who waited on the walk. She gave him a carved little grimace of recognition and imminent reproach as though she knew some bitter joke about everyone and everything. How had she known he would emerge at just that hour, how had she tracked him down before he had had time to compose an acceptable reason for his failure? He must meet the situation anyway, he must be kind, but this would have to be a conclusive scene. He must tell her he could do nothing for her, he would have to lop her off and drop her away from him into some vat of his own, the festering cloaca of life's irreconcilables, and he shuddered inwardly with echoes of the morning.

"*Madame*," he said, fumbling for words. "I saw the Consul this morning. He told me to tell you—" But he didn't need to finish for, with a look of arrogant fury, she wrested the story from him like a stolen belonging.

"You lie, *Monsieur*. You did not try. You believed him, not

173

me. You are worse than he is, because he does not pretend. He is cruel, but you only pretend to be kind." But suddenly the structure of her anger collapsed. "Forgive me, *Monsieur,* I was angry, I was disappointed. You will help me still, no? You will speak to the Consul again. You will not let him believe the lies."

But Dr. Woodley had backed away. He could do no more at the moment. It was six o'clock, the lowest hour of the evening. Above him the palms still swayed, revolving heads of clashing green knives that cut the sunset sky to bits and let in the dark. He walked to the bus stop, quickening his pace without seeming to run, while the frenzied old woman, now blurred in the twilight like an enormous brown hand waving at him, called out, "You are an American, *Monsieur.* You can do it if you will!" And she seemed indeed beyond her reason as she shouted the shibboleth of his nationality like the name of a god or devil in the contracting twilight.

Whatever finality, freedom, and sense of extrication Dr. Woodley carried to bed with him seemed not so certain in the queasy moments before breakfast, and when he emerged into the yellow morning light, there was Dona Carlota pacing back and forth before the columns, almost satisfying some perverse appetite of anticipation and prediction.

The "chase" was on. There was no doubt of it now. In the days that followed, Dr. Woodley was to wonder at his prowess in evasion, like a dexterity recovered from youthful games of "Cops and Robbers," as he dodged in and out of doorways, down out-of-the-way streets, taking cover in little frequented *botequims,* giving his pursuer the slip in a hundred artful ways. But he had not counted upon the resources nor the endurance of Dona Carlota. She was his shadow, his alter ego, the phantom of his other self. The possibility of deluding her became an absorbing consideration of each day, usually ending with their strange juxtaposition in some unpredictable place, a *cul-de-sac* of laughter or exasperation, according to the pressures of the moment.

174

If he met her going the other way, she wheeled around immediately as if drawn by a magnet inside his heart. Her schedule of
wandering could be adapted to his precise sense of time and
direction at a moment's notice, reminding him half humorously
of the old sentimental song of Rudy Vallee, "My Time Is Your
Time." Her "stickability" was maddening, and, in his bitterer
moments, he could have shaken her off like a leech that sought
some special syrup of his blood. In another mood, she appalled
him as a kind of inescapable human evidence from which he had
no right to flee "down the nights and down the days, down the
arches of the years, down the labyrinthine ways."

He might be walking in the Praça Paris on an amber afternoon when the landscape was held in a pause of gold, and there
was Dona Carlota streaking every clarity of air through which
she moved as though she expelled a potent, murky brown in-
cense, a trailing banner of the world's derangement. On Saturday, if he went to the Copacabana for a swim, he was aroused
from a sunbath by a rumbling blend of vituperation and sup-
plication and saw her stretch out beside him, very much at home
among the rocks and shells, almost whimsically aware that she
had caught him naked in the white and winter refinement of
his flesh.

Instead of riding on the bus, he took to catching the *bonde,* a
wild, open-air jungle cousin of the American streetcar, always
so loaded that the men hung along the sides like tatters of flesh
lacerated from its body, while their wives packed themselves
inside. Though he pushed deep into the womb of sullen women,
Dona Carlota managed a place not far from him, a squat figure
of opaque topaz among the soft neighboring flesh, and the
bonde rolled maniacally along while she "smoked him out," ex-
posing him to the concentric concentration of feminine displeasure. When he stepped from the infernal machine, he felt
himself hounded out of the human situation by shrill womanly
laughter and the sly smiles of the men.

Sometimes, though rarely, he would see her across the plaza,
lost in herself, having cut the umbilical attachment even to him.

175

She sat on a bench simmering obtusely in the heat, looser now, her clothing spattered with blood as from stoning and all awry, looking very much like a female Lear of the tropics as she clutched at her wisps of hair and buttoned and unbuttoned her coat. She had become indeed "the thing itself."

All the while another turn of the screw was being given by the invisible hands that controlled the University. The lectures were going even more badly and a distressing knowledge of failure plagued him and thwarted his excursions among accustomed pleasures. One afternoon toward the end of his two months' assignment after a particularly humiliating experience of delivering a hard-worked lecture on James to a token audience and an exasperating bout with Dona Carlota which, after long pursuit, had ended in the trap of a favorite bookstore, he took refuge in his room at the Gloria, dropping a load of newly-bound books on the bed without his usual care. His nook, at last, he said to himself, not far from a private indulgence in tears.

The room was delightful—there was some comfort in that. It was at the back of the hotel looking toward an impinging mountain, chosen for its closed, intimate, garden effect. His things were around him—even here he had made some progress as a connoisseur. There in the bookcases were his handsome, hand-bound volumes of French and Portuguese to which he had added today. On the wall, in the best light, hung a small Portinari, bought after much deliberation and financial misgiving, showing a flamboyant cock in the foreground and two brown-skinned natives touched by the shadow of red light, exquisite as surface decoration and yet having poignancy and depth in its folk yearning, the lyrical contrast between ruddy, natural exuberance and muted human suffering. Upon a shelf there was a glowingly carved saint from the old religious city of Bahia. In a drawer of his desk, heating it like a secret love, was a box containing a lovely aquamarine, which he was taking as a gift to the "beloved friend" whom circumstances had never quite permitted him to marry.

176

These few emblems and trophies of his faith made him long for his bachelor apartment in Evanston which was lined with books and decked with the treasures of his many tours. He would be home soon, thank God. The Brazilian venture had failed miserably. But why, why? He had come with the best of intentions and had tried to be finically conscientious in the discharge of his duties. But first there had been the trouble at the University and then this fanatical woman who would not let go. She had swollen in his consciousness out of all proportion from an annoying mote to a tumid bladder of disordered passions. When she came from Lisbon, she had left that tiny door of Europe open, trailing behind her the distempers of the time. Would it be the fate of the New World to wear such a macabre and strangling garland around its throat at War's end? Could it give everything that would be asked of it?

He thought of Virginia Woolf, another of his "authorities," who had recently committed suicide, prophesying, "All lovely things will be destroyed." He remembered Spengler's dire foreshadowings, his prediction of the return to "the brute blood of the world." He thought of the "monuments of unaging intellect," which in the mounting wash of horrors were tiny obelisks of marble, as pathetic as the white, upward-straining fingers of a drowning man.

It was the enormous sense of the breakdown of form in life which lay so heavily upon him, and somehow the whole, wild, dark emanation seemed to funnel through the unyielding tenacity of Dona Carlota. She was the frightening *avant garde* of the fauna of universal proliferation, the "lost link" between worlds, the slouching, slovenly, bruised, and pitiful embodiment of some terrible evasion. He felt for her and longed to feel more, wondering if somewhere along the line there had been a failure of sympathy. He had been willing to help her; he had tried. But had he tried enough? Had he given in too easily to the belief that she was beyond the pale? Yet, he asked himself, how can the heart be given everywhere? For through his blood he

177

could hear the slow seepage of the century which left one singularly drained and incapable of response, ending perhaps in a heart-castration, an impotence turned away from the baffling complexity of human life to the safety of insentience. And, at the pith of the noxious reverie, stood Dona Carlota like the incarnation of all his questionings, a residual, unaccommodated object, a leftover tossed down by God just when love reached an abstract and absolute purity.

A week later the door of the big Pan American plane closed on Dr. Woodley, and he was thankfully leaving Brazil forever though a mist of tears in his eyes made him marvel at how suffering endears. The downward suction of the take-off brought a faint nausea of regret, breaking off finally the entwining cords, leaving so many ruptured ends streaming in the wind. The last days had been most affecting. Some reservoir of pent feeling had been tapped, and there had been a round of good-bye parties, testimonial lunches and dinners, and the soft, encircling arm of Brazil had clutched him in a sudden *abraço* he would remember all his life. The University officials had appeared out of nowhere to thank him for a job well done, claiming him as a friend of international education, *bem querido,* and the students gave him a touching gift, timidly and unobtrusively, with the hesitancy of a little hand in a large one. The air which had seethed with devils shimmered with the wing-beat of another sort. The warmness of his nature responded fully, and he could have even wished for more time to stand under the burst of glory.

On the eve of departure, he had seen Dona Carlota seated at the edge of a fountain in the Praça like a cracked, earthen vessel, still talking aloud as though not to forget language. She saluted him with her indomitable spirit which amounted almost to gleefulness, striated by expressions of scorn and redoubtable anger, as she parroted her eternal performance: "Ah, *Monsieur,* the American! You are going to help me, no?" He had looked at her with a foolish feeling of affection like an old acquaintance, perhaps the oldest that he had. Now memory held her face longest

178

while the plane relinquished the dim outline of the great mountains as though she stood at the edge of the continent, permitting no farewell.

BOAT WITH
AN EYE OF GLASS

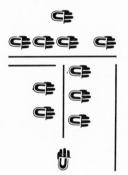

As the years go by, there is a person, or there are persons, never more than a few, to whom we attach a special, endearing and enduring significance. There are certain things we have done which maintain an aura so that they stand out along the cloudy corridor of days in niches of radiant posture, a hall of heroes hidden in the mind, and each figure in that aureate concavity is a wonderful blending of ourselves with that which was, like a dual marble of the sympathy and substance of our past. It is thus that we gather perspective, acquiring treasures as we go along, keeping a light before the special acquisition by the devotion of our feeling for it in that time past. As the world around us tells us that we walk forward, there is an ever more alluring tendency to turn the head and, in an aggressive retrospect, recapture and relume the inspired moments of the progression saying, "That's how we were together, that was the place, those were the days."

I remember such a person, a time, and place in the Rio of 1923 when I was twenty-two.

But first let me yield the present to you, and leave myself all the freer to move around among things remembered. It is 1943, and I am on my way to Brazil again. If it had not been for the War, I probably would not have made the trip, but with the idea of Death as the great protagonist, gathering the world like supernumeraries into its magnetic scene, I felt the irresistible urge of the antagonist to recover an intensity of life I knew I

183

had experienced in Rio. Moreover there was the memory of Raul, the prototype of friendship, the young Faustus of my more timid seeking, that beckoned to me as though a dark world must be balanced with the light if the poise of humanity were to be maintained.

I spent a good many sleepless nights over the decision, but I suppose unconsciously I had been longing to return for such a long time as not to have been able to allow myself another refusal. There were Doris and the children to consider—only one air priority was allowable—they would have to stay in New York, increasing my sense of guilt for what might have seemed a romantic "flying down to Rio" in a time of crisis, though Washington had connected my trip with the war effort. As an executive of Standard Oil, I was to put through a deal on oil rights which our office in Rio had been slowly attempting to accomplish against local opposition. However, it was not until Doris urged me to go that I convinced myself it was "important" —Doris, standing at the window looking far away, acknowledging this Southern longing in me as a floating vision that rose in a bubble of sea-colors and clashing palm fronds, something ineluctable and yet insubstantial between us, present and then gone, a release of images in search of a body, haunting and chimaerical.

Then when my doctor permitted me to go only on the condition that I combine business with a rest, I rather happily canceled my air passage in favor of the long sea voyage, once again freed by Doris to go alone, glad of being able to savor the slow ecstasy of approach, hoping to lose some of the armor and encumbrance of the years en route, as though the boat would leave New York ponderously and glide into the harbor of Rio as lithe as a wind-honed bird. The long contemplative hours on the ocean would be those of a devotee. It would be a novitiate, a cleansing time, as I prepared to reclaim the tropic of my youth.

For through the years that was what Rio had become to me— the visionary South of all my snow-bound Northern yearning, the fructive center of the earth's body, the pith of appetite, the climate of blessed mornings and benign evenings, the luxuriant frontier of Adventure that blooms at the edge of Order. The whole city had opened in my desire like an enormous loose flower, and there, like the heart of it all, was the island of Paquetá where Raul had taken me so often, which now in the depth of recall rose free of all the rest whenever I could summon this sunken realm of the South. For, in my waking hours, it was as submerged and buried that it appeared to me. It was not unlike a purer Pompeii of my youthful pleasure which some dark eruption in the soul threatened forever, changing in mid-air its flake of fire into reminiscent petals, muffling the island of bougainvilleas with the purple ash of memory.

Only in sleep was there motion and pliant life, seen in a glass-bottomed boat from above, the world of flowers bending and rippling in the current of dream like hands of enticement waving beneath transparence, the boat, white, functional, mechanical, a naked body of odious progression, struck with tremor, as though a mounting underswell were surging below that might lift the hard instrument of surface motion and break it across the purple pinnacle of flowers.

Though I speak of lurid dreams, I am not a man given to hallucinations. I think I know what is dream and what is reality —the magnetic counter-pull of the one and the other has never sent me dizzy and reeling as it has with so many of my contemporaries. I have indulged in fantasy during the free times which I have allowed myself, but I have conquered the world around me as well—I am socially competent, I am culturally congruent. Doris, I believe, would tell you that, for she has helped me to weld the pattern. I got my start as an office boy with Standard Oil in Rio where, tired of college, I had gone to knock around and make a man of myself with youth's vague hunger for knowing and doing everything once. Through the years I prospered, and now have my name on a letterhead and all that goes with it.

Doris would tell you that I am "solid and substantial," for she has a proud faith in my supremacy and endurance and surely a need to believe in them. I would like to show her sometimes what I call my "island smile," the look of the free floater, but I wonder how it would go with the well-tailored suits which she considers so becoming to me, the well-tended manners, and my self-containment so carefully preened. I suppose with my height and dark hair, only slightly graying, my well-trimmed moustache, and compact look of health, I am what you would call somewhat "impressive," although in the morning when I shave, that face does not always seem to belong entirely to me. Though I have no delusions about my identity, strongly rooted as I think I am in the world of reality, there is a revolving expression in my eyes, bewildering me as those turning doors in hotels did when I was a child. I am not always sure what look I am going to show the others, although I am constantly, and I must say gladly, reminded that the wheel of introspection turns only for me. Doris never lets me think that she is aware, and I should be unhappy to think that she were, for I have stood her scrutiny for nearly fifteen years.

Though she has accepted this almost ghostly fume above our common life, this ectoplasm of unshared experience, it would not have been pleasant for her to see through my eyes, standing as I often do on a late winter afternoon in the library of our house in Beekman Place, melting the world of snow outside with the sunlight of another climate in my reverie, casting a tableau of purple and rose against the backdrop of white. But I often do just that, sensing her behind me as she enters the room, appraising my presence, taking the columnar view of me. Sometimes, as in the earlier days, I long to turn and run quickly toward her, and, in spite of the heavy pediment of our lives, stand close to her and let her see the hollowness behind the sheen, the tube without the core of valor, and share whatever doubt she hides behind her strength.

But I am wary of my knowledge of Doris. I am not sure whether she understands me, nor really whether I understand her in any growing, developing sense of personality. I have merely decided what she thinks of me and what I probably think of her.

186

It would frighten me to test this postulate of Man and Wife by the standard of a resurgent and aggressive love which would, I am afraid, appear so primitive to her. For she does not seem to need me in this personal way any more. Whenever there is friction, she recites from her long dossier of respect for me, and I am left with nothing but an elegiac mood. As for my sons, Marshall, Jr., and Henry, I have learned not to be too possessive, and they, in turn, have accepted me merely as a necessary presence. Yet, sometimes when they stand before the fire with their mother, flanking the image of her golden good looks like little eidolons of protective concern, I seem to detect an accusation in their scrutiny as though their eyes had caught that turning flicker in my face.

But the drift of our lives moves with the utmost efficiency— our house is a machine for living. Doris has a schedule for everything, and I abide by the checklist, for I can find nothing vulnerable in her way of doing things. And so we stand evenly balanced in the scales, Doris with the strange and almost threatening power of her decorum, her strength of will, and I through a weight that is attributed to me as head of the family, though I wish that one of us would be weighed in the balance and found wanting, perhaps both of us in different ways, but I cannot shift one milligram of this equipoise of "gracious living."

So in a time of death, I am glad to be on my way, New York left behind, humped high with the rock of its buildings like the Stonehenge of a modern, manic race. As we go along in life, so much of the good, it seems to me, comes to us as recovery of what has been lost. When we are young, we have the sense of walking forward with confidence, and the backward look is unthinkable. So it was with Raul and me—we let out our minds like streamers at a masquerade, and if they fell in colorful chains around us, we broke through them with the exuberance of another faith. I remember how we thought that life could be summed up, understood, and contemplated in lucid adoration.

But in the darkening irony of maturity, so it seems, the Great Questions of our youth become vaster and the powers of heart and mind lose their projectility in a smaller, weakening, dwindling flare. So now I am taking "a walk," as they would say in New York—this voyage is like a leisurely stroll toward a world I believe has never changed. I am going back to meet Raul—this trip is a sort of homage to him. I think of him coming toward me with outstretched hand as though we were meeting on the docks before embarking for Paquetá. Though he died not long after I left Brazil and was, I am told, buried on the island, I discard that realization. I do not wish to believe in the mortality of his world.

It has been a pleasant voyage, a long sustained anticipation of a personal Paradise. The boat moved slowly at first, hard and encasing, menacing as a destroyer ready to change its colors in mid-journey, then moving more quickly, sloughing its defensive shields, seeming less mechanical, gliding at last on the motion of jettisoned regrets. I love a harbor city better than all others. I like the way it drinks the waters of the world and how it gives itself as channel and passage, acknowledging the incoming and outgoing, using the imperceptible net of its soul to sieve the motions of men. When you are next there, in a town by the water, notice the exquisite sense of flow which plays over you like a crystalline current of time's dreaming, taking all but the best you have loved in its lustral wash, leaving a sense of your own essence until you know that this cleanliness and purity of line are what you have wanted all your life. As we pass through the gates of the mountains, I know again that Rio is my harbor city—not New York where I seemed far from the water, the harbor throat so gorged and throttled that though the great beaker was tilted, I waited and was thirsty.

But now all pent dreaming is set free. The color-vent of the mind from which the bubbles of fantasy float up is closed. There is no necessity for it. I do not need to look down at the deck of the ship and see if it is glass. I feel that I am below the world to which I had become accustomed, and am in that motion which I had found only in dream. I see Paquetá in the distance, and whatever vacuum remains is filled with my past which must be present again. I think of Raul, and I know that when I am in the city and then, most finally, on the island again, I will have the sense of a complete connection like a handclasp merging two continents of life. The last moments before we dock are spent thinking of him whom I must not lose for I have come too far in order to be sure that I remember. There is something agonizing in my feelings as though the mind were a fumbling sorcerer who could not quite bring off the transformation of recall, but I persist. I close my eyes and shut out everything but memory. I see Raul on the dock with his hand extended and his wonderful smile of comradeship.

It is Saturday, no work to be done, we are going to the island, and he stands there near the rail a little impatiently, not wanting us to miss the boat. He is my friend, and I never think of how he looks when I am with him, but today I pause and take a mental picture, partly out of guilt at being late, wanting to register the gentle, though unsentimental, way he greets me, partly from a belief in "recording" which comes over me now and then. He is dressed in a navy blue, sleeveless sweater, white ducks, sneakers, and carries a package of lunch under his arm. His coloring is dark, but his eyes are a luminous gray, intensified by a tendency of pallor in the face. He looks frailer than I, and I remember with a twinge that he is an arrested tubercular. I can hardly believe it because of his vitality, and it is the one thing that makes him seem remote from me, as though he knew another dimension of experience which I have been denied.

On the ferry going over, Raul, whom I call "Ray" to bring him closer to my American comprehension, is everywhere, dragging me along, as always. He shows me every corner of the boat, speaks to all the people, with particular friendliness to the farmer folk who sit lumped together, ill at ease, their city purchases stacked around them. He tells me to speak to them and I do so in my pidgin Portuguese, glad to see their weathered faces crack into smiles.

189

I suppose this is why I like Ray—he reveals myself to me—
he assures me that I can do, would like to do, so many things that
I have denied myself. He makes me believe in my rapport with
the world around me.

We are nearing Paquetá, "our island," to which we come as
often as we can. We go everywhere in Rio together. We have
girl friends in common, we go to parties together, but we like
the island best. Ray, though, never thinks of it as "enough"—
he loves the city passionately too. For him the effect of the island
is lapidary, taking away the rough edges of daily living, but,
finally, too detached, inward-looking, and self-centered.

We rent bicycles at the dock, and are off at a leisurely pace,
riding through the little town which has yielded itself to flowers.
The bougainvillea is everywhere, the main flower-tone of the
island, purple and rose, leaving the subtler accents of color to
the smaller flowers so that one remembers them throughout the
day like piquant contrasts of a predominant mood.

"Let's stop here, Marsh," Ray says a dozen times. And he
breaks off and hands me sprigs of a little, gaping, yellow flower
with a big name, *bôca de leão,* lion's mouth, and in the condensation of imagined sound, there is a tiny roar across the morning. I who have known flowers only as familiar now find them
intimate. From another bank he brings me a *brinco da prin-
cessa,* earring of the princess, a pendent red flower which seems
to hang from the invisible form of a girl. He, the native, is
helping me to see his country through the eyes of a stranger. As
he keeps showing me the flowers, I do not feel foolish about it
after a while, for they are as alive to him as people or animals.

We move on, talking to many people along the way, asking
directions helplessly, and I notice how helplessness is so attractive to everyone. We talk with the peasant girls especially, and
Ray knows how to treat them with a caressive courtesy. They
laugh at his jokes and take no offense. We go for a swim, we
climb the hills, we are a cartwheel of color and motion along
the winding white sand roads. We pause on a bluff overlooking
the water to talk and later to eat lunch. I reflect on our rapport,

190

and I know that whether we admit it or not most of us like the idea of friendship between foreigners, as though sincerity among them were easier.

I look at Ray. He is tired; there is a shadow in his face. It makes me think of his illness which he never discusses but which broods about him in repose like a dark, attendant mother. I wonder if it is from her that he has learned such joy. I listen in the shadow-tarnished air for some message that he hears and I do not. He is pensive and quiet, then gleams across to me as though he had heard some news of Now which I do not know. He is the young prophet of Now; he has a way of judging that I do not know.

"Marsh," he says impulsively. "I've been thinking a lot about you today. You're the best friend I have, you know. You think me rather wonderful, I can tell that. I'm not, of course, but you see me that way. And that's what matters. I'm going to miss you terribly when you go, you old son of a gun. You will go, of course. And you should. You really belong back there." He pushed against the air as though opening a door. "You know, I think of even friendship as being provisional, although I don't like that word. It mustn't bind, it mustn't hold back. If we like our friends, we must know how to let them go. They are like clouds, I often think. We mustn't love them any less because the wind is in them and they move."

I do not agree with him though I let him think so. He has awakened me to Now, and I am caught in its shimmering net. I do not want it to change, to pass. I do not acknowledge his resolution of love and the flux of things. I resent this flowing away of the world, this Now that I have come to love so much. Though my mind is given to the concept that "the One remains," my heart denies it, clinging to "the Many that fade and pass." Even in the full joy of Now, I resist. I long to put ramparts against change around me while Ray stands in the rainbow stream of time like a filter of its beauty. Already he seems a phantom to me, and I think of his illness with terror, but I will not believe in his death which he accepts so calmly as

191

though it has become a particularly radiant way of looking at life.

On the boat going home, I am full of controlled sadness and nostalgia, whereas Ray once again moves happily about among the others. I lean over the railing and watch the wake of the boat as it churns a huge foamy braid of dying color, and I think of it as holding in tow forever the purple island behind us, a rope which I have not been able to sever, though Ray shows me that it is possible, for he moves on, unmoored, neither imprisoned by things nor enslaving them. That's it—he takes the Now with him, while I leave it behind. Is it those alone who have something eternal to live for who know how to say farewell?

Today I am here. It is my first morning in Rio, not yet the island but the grand vestibule of embarkation, and I love it. I have come back from a long trip to a city full of greetings. There are so many here, like me, who belong to the time I love, who have perhaps saved it and stored it in the present-past forever. There's Helena Soares, Bibi Guedes, Henrique Paranagua, Carlos Bandeira, and many others. I think of their vital wreath of friendship which belongs to Ray and me.

But first I want to look around. I don't want to see anyone until I am entirely *in situ*. There's my work to do, of course, the contacts to be made, but I do these rapidly, efficiently, with blinders on, sealed in a tube of aggressive action. I do not let it set up conflicts; it is water rushing through concealed pipes in an abundant system of its own. It creates power for its own ends, it belongs to itself alone. There is no feeling in that part of me which it uses as a duct.

I am staying at the Gloria, and I like its dignified, traditional elegance which has been old-fashioned for a long time. It is an architectural time-pause which assures me that what I am looking for is here. During all my free hours I wander through the streets of the city with expectation, the old streets first, the Rua do Ouvidor, which is unchanged. I have the sense of looking for someone in the crowd and wonder if the next corner will bring us bumping against each other. But then, as I walk along, I have a slightly sickening sense of being utterly alone. I cannot seem to see in the way that I believe. Never before have I had such a feeling of insubstantiality. I lean against the side of a building to bruise memory into my being as the stuff of Now, for I feel the narrow abyss of the street that contains the stream of people in which I have drenched myself as a reviving baptism crumble and fade away, leaving me in a spatial desert which I must rebuild and repopulate with the eyes of change. It is as though I were a god on a plateau of nothingness and the great burden were mine. I must build a city, and I must sire a people.

Though I am not given to panic, and I know this is just a mood, I return in a state of exhaustion to the Gloria. I sit in a chair on the terrace looking toward Sugar Loaf, whose contours are like a shape of Forever, and across the blue water which changes only in terms of itself. The vista of the ocean makes me think of Doris, for only last anniversary I gave her an aqua-marine which was like a congealed solution of its enchantment. At twilight, as her white hand moved in the dark, I used to watch it dartling the blue beacon of a world I could not forget. I wonder if she ever suspected that it was an amulet she wore for me.

I remember how much I have talked to her about Rio and that talking to her helped to insure me of its reality. We have spent so many evenings together on a couch looking at photographs, joint custodians of their vivid story. Perhaps the reliquary atmosphere began to bore her after a while. The night she got up in the middle of a film about Rio I was showing to some friends and slipped into her bedroom, where I found her weeping and complaining of a headache, convinced me that was so. I think she knew I never quite forgave her. Nevertheless, I half wish that she were here with me. Could she have helped, I ask myself, today on that plain when the sides of the world fell away?

The waiter brings me a Scotch and soda. I sip it slowly, feeling very much myself in the dreariest way possible without anyone

193

around as the *bête noire* of it all. This entire voyage seems the most fantastic fiction of my life, a story that threatens to take the narrative thread in hand and loop it into some perversely knotted ending. This is the five o'clock slump, I tell myself. It will pass. What I need is a trip to the island. Before I see any of the others, I determine to go. Yes, tomorrow.

I feel good this morning. It is an exquisitely clear day for crossing to Paquetá. On the boat going over, the old wing-feeling of moving toward pleasure is with me again. I conjure up the presence of two young men who are off on a lark, hungrily devouring every moment of time without a niggard trace in their affections. I am myself. I am Ray. I am clear as the morning in my feelings; they are a passageway again; the world flows through them, and look—I am holding nothing back! The strong pull of the island is in my blood. I am going back to Now, I am recovering what I should never have left behind. I am a man in search of the present. I believe it exists on the island.

Suddenly I am disturbed. Nearby there are two young soldiers, an American and a Brazilian, in their brown and green uniforms, talking and laughing. They are braided together in friendship that swings free in the motion of time. The young American has learned some Portuguese and the Brazilian a few sentences of English; they are talking about girls, games, and the War, in bright, dashing phrases. They are on a jaunt; they are making the best of time. The Brazilian is probably a member of the Expeditionary Force soon to be sent across; one of them, perhaps both, will die before it is all over. Their voices strike my reverie with the lash of a scourge and leave it in tatters. They have burst through its silken tympanum like wayward clowns who mock everything but the moment's moment. They live in a zenith-world of happiness which is ruthless without knowing that it is so.

The rising sound of their voices lifts a great wave of the War above me, a brilliant, curving thrust that would inundate and

194

capsize the boat. But they are riding the crest, buoyant at the point they will remember all their lives. I think of the down-sweep when they have rushed over the hump of excitement and happiness. I think of afterwards which is the greatest trap of all. I think of those, like these young men perhaps, who will win the short war and lose the long one. I see their wave of happiness above me; it has a classic gleaming light upon it; I listen, as in a tragedy, for the thump of its impact as it flattens on the leveling shore.

I look up and see the buffer-mouth of the pier looming to-ward me and brace myself for the collision I have longed for. The island is mine at last! I have forgotten the War for the mo-ment as I let myself be spawned with the crowd into the island stillness. It is only when they have all vanished as through exits in a scene that I am forced to admit that I am here to play it all alone. The island awaits the great, good words of the protag-onist, for such now have I become. It listens for the soliloquy which I alone can speak. There is an indescribable solemnity here, gravely beautiful, but without the sparkle I remember, like a jewel turning in the sun. I see that the island lies in a kind of eternal quiescence—everywhere there is a sense of wait-ing.

I know I must walk to the little cemetery where Ray is buried, and I do so slowly, with the curious sense of fictive movement. I believe that the radiance I lack is Ray's to give me again. If I can be sure that he is inviolable, that what he has become in diminuendo can return in the full diapason of memory, I will know that I am right, that where we were alive, we are alive.

It is a windless day, there is no motion anywhere but my own. The banks of bougainvillea, rose and purple, rise above me, encircle and enclose me, no longer seen from above, pliant and swaying, in the longing remoteness of a glass-bottomed boat. I am "down-under," I am within. I have come home to Now. The ceaseless prowling motion of the boat is over.

But, suddenly, there is a tremor of the wind, petals fall in a purple ash around me, and I look up as from a depth into the descending whirls, so thick that they would seem to bury me in their death of flowers. Here is the casting on of petals, I think, with an awakening sense of escape, and I look down at Ray's grave to yield him from it, but the earth is secure and sealed with the light of morning shining above it, and all that I think I see on the bright surface of the grass is the reflection of myself. I have come a long way to pay such homage. I feel like a man who has watched a tyrant laid to rest.

Now that I know, I can leave, for Ray has won again. He has expelled me forever from the island as he tried to do so long ago. He has brought me to that point where he lived his life with the sense of death around it. He has opened that final dimension of our friendship to me. He has taught me to hear the dark, attendant mother who speaks lest we starve in the midst of fullness, who tells us that to be able to live we must know how to die. I shall never forget the Now of all that lovely past for it has taught me at last to want to live again, and I know that that is what memory is for.

I think of Doris and her patience—now I see it—her unfaltering dedication to the world as it is. I think of New York, that massive pressure of man, built against the Unanswered and Unknown, straining mightily, sometimes obtusely, but convinced that in some mysterious way it lies at the edge of radiance. Perhaps it is not too late, perhaps there is still time, I tell myself, as though I have discovered the oldest and youngest strength of man, words to be spoken by the protagonist above the chorus that reminds: There was a boat with an eye of glass.

BRASIL MORENO

Buck Matthews gave the inward sigh of a man who thinks he has found a new friend. They had been talking only a few minutes, but he could already sense her as a resting place, and he was willing to be inclosed by her, the milling crowd around them in the room now like vague shapes beyond glass windows. The Director of the Instituto Brasil—Estados Unidos wedged in between them at intervals as though she were a shopkeeper interested in rearranging the mannequins, but when she left they healed together again.

The girl was Léa Fontes, recently returned from the States where she had graduated from Smith. Buck noticed her immediately for she seemed to be the only one there who had come without social anticipations. She was dressed attractively, simply, as she might have for herself, on an evening at home, and her face was lightly made up, making her look almost like a foreigner among the other Brazilian girls with their heavy *maquilhagem* laid on in a disguising mask and the affectations of their dress which restrained whatever simple humanity their bodies might have breathed into the room.

She had perhaps, Buck decided, the look of what he had been searching for during the three months since his arrival—the classic Brazilian face which he had not found among the Negroes or muddy mulattoes, the earth-folk, nor among the *gran finos* who were, as the name implied, the distilled products of world urbanity. He wanted what Brazil—the land, the climate, the racial soul, if such a thing there were—was trying to produce: the honesty of its best human effort. To him, always in search of the ideal, she appeared to represent "Brasil moreno," brown Brazil . . . or was it dark Brazil, grown from an Old World planting, calling out of the air a new name? Europe was there —there was no doubt about it—the Portuguese adventure. This heritage was evident in her brunette hair and the skin under which a dark current seemed to ripple. Her eyes, a tawny brown, had a sun-shade in them, casting a shadow over her features which were sharp, almost pointed, yet somehow soft and subtly dimpled, faintly resembling the portrait of an early Madonna. She was, Buck declared to himself, "wholesome," although, applied to her, the word had its *chiaroscuro,* like gold lying in shadow, and not at all what it meant at home with the lovely, lucid girls through whom you could see the sun, the sky, and the world beyond.

Perhaps it was Buck's look of not belonging echoed in Léa's face that had moved them toward each other across the room so that gradually he pulled her to his side through the suction of revolving people like a girl on a rope. Perhaps it was his Navy Lieutenant's uniform—he later discovered her father was an Admiral of the Brazilian Navy. In any case they were soon standing together, balancing their teacups, hanging on to each other by the arrestment of determined attraction. What will the human race ever do about preliminaries, Buck thought to himself, and, as usual, handed the matter over helplessly to his companion who, like most women, would probably know how to grasp some stray wisp of conversation to which they could both cling until something could be said for the moment and of the moment. It was Léa's beautiful simplicity, he noticed, that enabled her to recognize how difficult it was for him to meet people easily, sensing in him perhaps some intense, lonely effort to belong to himself. Before the tea was over, there had been a graceful exchange of biographies, and he was to come for dinner the following night. Buck marveled at the fine compact package of beginning friendship which she handed him with her good-night words.

Yet, in the bus on the way back to the apartment which he shared with three other officers, he held back a little from it all. He was taking lessons in Portuguese at the Institute and he had come to the get-together rather aimlessly to meet some people, but now, as always, he was not quite sure. Here was someone who promised to be a friend—already she had asked him for dinner. Perhaps that was the trouble. It seemed too sudden— there was always his damned tendency toward withdrawal, not shyness which was mainly superficial, but distrust of becoming involved. His status as a Communication's officer in the Naval Attaché's office was uncertain. He could be shipped out at a moment's notice, and he had decided long ago not to entangle anyone unfairly.

On the other hand, he was lucky to have found a friend like Léa so soon. His opinion of himself was not too high, or rather it was mingled constantly with the conception of himself as he thought he should be. If he had been willing to describe his personality, he might have said that he was one of those "who walk between." He was not ugly, stupid, dull, but neither could he grant himself their handsome and glowing opposites. He had sandy hair, faded blue eyes, a good build, and an amiable look —nothing more that he could claim. Nevertheless the girls liked him, he was sure of that, making him sometimes wonder if the conception of colorless mediocrity to which he had resigned himself were altogether true. It was he who had always let the girls go, giving them nothing very definite to hang on to, fading away from them in conversation as though he did not hear or see them very well once it became apparent that they were willing to slow him down enough to congeal him into an image they desired. No, he was not to be had in effigy, not even by himself, certainly not by the molding hand of a woman who did not really know his substance.

It was the acquisitive type that a man like himself feared, he concluded, stepping down from the bus and walking wearily toward the apartment house with its dark entrance set in a heavy yawn as though he returned to a world of ponderous disinterest. It was someone wanting him just as he was that he recoiled from, wanting to give herself as she was, willing to settle for nothing, to make an alliance on the basis of so little. The world was full of "child marriages" between people who would spend the rest of their lives limiting each other, holding each other back, fearing to permit the release of the captive in the other.

As he climbed into bed, he could hear the breathing of his roommates who lay there in the dark like islands of contented humanity peopled with iridescent dreams while the motion of his coming sleep seemed nothing but the stream of time itself without this moorage, this pacific accretion of body and mind which was Ned, Tim, and Jake as they lay anchored to the last joy and comfort of their present lives. He could only smile at them, for he wished them well, as in sleep he drifted round in a winding swoon until images of islands were stirred, crushed, and dissolved in the mortar of the night by a great hand that used his body like a pestle to bruise and bray the compound of the given into another blend of being.

The dinner at Léa's house in the Urca section of Rio was Buck's first introduction to traditional Brazil. He had been to the home of a few of the *gran finos,* decorated in styles of Paris or New York, and he was not prepared for the dark heaviness, the old-fashioned formality of the Fontes house: white stucco roofed with red tile conforming to a natural world of continual sunlight, but making no effort inside to conceal its soul, furnished with ponderous, durable, jacarandá furniture, elaborately carved and scrolled. The tone was one of quiet brooding, the massive chairs, tables, sofas, not unlike kneeling and crouching animal forms that had gathered around the human in a kind of fatalistic waiting.

The front door opened into the dining room, the center of

202

family living in houses of this type, he learned later on, an architectural trait inherited perhaps from a working people to whom food meant a climactic hour and who renewed their bodies and their humanity in the same place. Léa hurried him into a charming patio—sitting room at the back of the house, a frothy, gay, indoors-outdoors room with touches of tropic color, nuances of Portugal, France, and here and there the stamp of American college life. With its cheerful international effect, he could see it must be her creation. It didn't deny the rest of the house; it merely floated out of it like the exhalation of a fanciful dream which the dark body of the interior released.

Léa looked lovely in a burnished dress that blended with her brown hair and eyes, her honey-colored skin. After they had an introductory drink alone, the Admiral and his wife came in, a ceremonious pair with circles around their eyes like issuing rings of inner darkness, dressed in black, giving subtle little smiles and restrained gestures to the guest in lieu of English which they did not speak, followed by apologetic asides to Léa in Portuguese. Laura, the younger sister, came in late accompanied by her *namorado,* a dark, lush, beach-boy type. With her blondined hair and slangy English, she made Buck shudder at how tawdry the "American way" could be, superimposed upon a different kind of soul, but he noticed that Léa was not ashamed of her, seeing it perhaps as normal that the real expatriate is the one who stays at home.

At dinner, the talk turned to politics—Léa had been a history and government major at Smith—and the whole family leaned forward with interest, while she acted as passageway for the conversation.

"You know, we are not pro-Vargas, Buck," she said, and her father nodded his head vigorously. "We've never been for the Estado Novo—it's an absolute dictatorship. It takes everything for itself and leaves nothing for the people."

"But the people love it, Léa," Buck said. "That's what we Americans hear on all sides. Getulinho, the friend of the workers. Vargas, the *Papai* of the poor."

"Nothing but propaganda," she answered bitterly. "Getulio controls everything, the army, the press. He is the *Estado Novo*. Those who might do something about it, the *gran finagem*, are on his side as long as he lets them alone. What can a poor peasant in Bahia do about it? He does not read, or write; he will never in all his life get to Rio. He will die like an animal in the jungle, and not a word he has ever said, a thought he could ever think, will reach further than the ears of his wife and a few friends like him."

Buck noticed that the entire family listened to her almost reverently as though she delivered a little sermon which they had prepared together earlier in their own tongue. No one tried to interrupt, not even Laura, as she continued.

"In the United States words carry, blend, make a big noise— there is truly a Voice of America. Here the people have no voice. They would like to cry out, it's true—in Manaus, Bahia, Matto Grosso—but the world is overwhelming down here. There's too much to do, so no one does anything. No wonder the sound of a Brazilian is a sigh. Sometimes at night it seems to me that I can hear them everywhere, the voices that sigh and accept. You will never understand what it is to be a Brazilian, Buck, until you understand how big, unmade, and even hostile this country is to the human being. No wonder it makes most of us lazy, resigned, always a little sad, and a few of us terribly ruthless."

"I suppose the answer is education. I understand there is about 80 per cent illiteracy down here," he said with unintentional sententiousness, for, confronted by Léa's earnestness, he felt at a loss.

"Yes," she said. "That and better health and better living conditions so that the mind can have a chance. You see the tropics are hateful to man in a way. They will not let him be himself. They give him without asking an easy, bare subsistence and demand only his submission. The Brazilian is trapped by nature which kills nothing in him but his spirit. The Earth-Mother is too strong here. She will not let us go. Do you know what I mean, Buck?"

204

She turned to him and he summoned his most sympathetic look in the hope of helping her along. It seemed to give her the final impetus she needed.

"You see," she continued, "I believe that man is happy only when he can feel that he has mastered his environment. People rave about Rio, but they never realize how imprisoning the spectacular can be."

"I never thought of it that way. It's the sort of thing we Americans never realize, I'm afraid," he said. "We're a little obtuse about other people anyway—or maybe just too self-centered. Most of us come down here on a holiday. Sort of like going to Hawaii. Have fun with the girls, see the pretty views, enjoy a world made out of flowers. Since that's what we come looking for, that's what we find. *Toujours gai,* you know."

"But there is gaiety here, Buck. What you don't see is that it's a kind of courage in the dark. It's the laugh in place of a sigh. It's blowing bubbles in the face of fate. If we can't be men, we can be children and pretend it doesn't matter."

As the dinner ended, Buck felt very close to the family. They didn't belong, they were like him, even though, of course, there were differences, perhaps even great ones which he would discover later. For the moment, he didn't care. He saw how lonely they must be—they wanted something better. They were not the people, they were not with those in power, but were shut off and lived almost in a little country of their own, accepting it with gentle nostalgia.

"Buck, don't look so serious. You're not a Brazilian," Léa finally said with a charming smile. "Just remember, we're not giving up. We've got a lot of endurance. We have to. We're like the old *baiana* who told her little boy who wanted to do everything at once, '*Calma, calma, meu filho, a terra é nossa*—Patience, patience, my son, the earth is ours.' "

Laura and her friend had gotten up abruptly, as though feeling left out, and Léa continued, "Oh, yes, Buck, I'd nearly forgotten. Laura and I want to take you dancing at the Urca. It might be fun to blow a few of those bubbles I was talking about."

They reached the Urca a few minutes before the first show and immediately went out on the floor to dance. It was a shadowy nightclub with the indirect glow of muted lights emanating from its walls like a promise of dawn seeping in. Buck, an easy and natural dancer, had already mastered the samba, finding that it was the first thing that really connected him with Brazil. Léa was an expert, and their steps synchronized perfectly to the slow samba the orchestra was playing, a braided music, he decided, a song of several strands, African, Indian, Portuguese, the blent life-tones of Brazil.

Though the floor was crowded, dancing was easy. It was the only dance he had run across which could be performed in one place, spaciousness achieved through subtle steps taken on top of each other and little changes of bodily position, the dancers loosely, commodiously rooted, swaying back and forth with the vegetal bending of the natural world. Léa felt willow-limber in his arms, and soon the room and the world beyond were swaying. When the atmosphere was saturated with the sound of music, the time was right for an individual effort, the climactic flare of motion, and Eros Volusia, the Urca's featured dancer, swept out to the front of the stage.

"That's Brazil, Buck!" Léa said with a happy, excited little cry. "Look at her!"

At the sound of Léa's voice, Buck felt his first strong desire for the Brazilian earth and somehow associated it in his mind with her who was this and yet was more. He shifted his eyes toward her constantly as he watched Eros sway back and forth, striking the friction of her flesh against the air until her body became a brown earth-flame in a jungle on fire, keeping all of her gestures somehow within the containing mood of the music, the plant-motion of Brazil . . . *Brasil moreno* . . . as he kept saying to himself.

When the dance was over, they returned to the floor and bent back and forth in the undulating rhythm of a landscape after a storm, rippling in a coalescent, healing breeze of diminuendo.

206

He could hear the leaf-noise of other dancers around him. His own words went softly into Léa's ear, and their whispering, the sinuosity of their bodies, was like the talk of trees.

He went home feeling that he could "sleep in the earth" forever, having felt earth-hands at his roots, somewhat troubled by this feeling, but sleeping with it as with destiny. When he woke the next morning, he felt rumpled as though he had slept in a tornado of dreams which had taken a good part of his mind and memory with it, leaving him his sensations of being lashed, torn, but still rooted—"out of uniform," he would have called it, and he said to himself, "Look here, Buck, old man. Get hold of yourself."

He looked out of the window into the Guanabara where in playful mania he had often wished to see the ships of all the navies of the world, so enormous it was, cupped around by blue-purple hills like a mixing bowl of God who might stir them together with His hand, those craft who knew the secret surface of all the oceans, and make the Ship, the great white carrier that epitomized the sailor's longing. He noticed that an American destroyer was at anchor in the harbor. Its battle gray turned dazzling in the sunlight, it floated like a mammoth, gleaming club impregnating the blue fern of the wind-ruffled water with its lordly power and precision of intent. It made him proud—the ship was magnificent, a triumph of intellect, drive, and what he would have called "masculine aesthetics," but it also made him think of the hard admiralty of so many he knew—the American Navy man could be one of the hardest and toughest men in the world. Some of us do have the Hawaiian complex, he said to himself. We treat them like children. We think we can drop them through our fingers like blossoms. We have no respect for them. They are like a woman we would make love to and never marry.

What followed the evening at Léa's was something he remembered as "the wonder-ball of days," for these weeks came back to him later in the image of a novelty which had been sent to

207

him as a child when he was sick: a big, compact affair composed
of lengths of white wrapping shedding gifts until it was unwound to its precious core where the gift of gifts lay like the
heart of the giver's bounty and affection. It seemed to him that
Léa was making such a gift for him, perhaps for herself as well,
wound around their lives to be unraveled during some future
sickness of the heart, themselves to be discovered at the pith of
it like two figurines from whose flesh billowed the convolutions
of an enchanted world. There was the trip to Paquetá, the little
flower-smothered island in the harbor; moonlight sailing on the
Lagõa; the sparkling days of a weekend in the mountains;
"island hunting" again; and always more dancing, the adhesive
force, "the cry of Brazil."

They talked about everything, and Buck discovered in her
what he called *tendresse,* since he did not know it as American
and had not yet discovered it as Brazilian. It was a woman's
predisposition to harmony, not unconnected with the feminine
passion for order, neatness, rightness among the affections, as
though her fingers were more agile than a man's in putting
together the mosaic of congeniality. She had a mind of her
own, but she was looking for its counterpart; she wanted not a
comrade but a lover, someone whose contrasting physical and
mental value could be the catalyst of her own. Men fight each
other, he learned from her, to bring out conflicts, either creative
or destructive, whereas a man and a woman sort out the pieces
which explode from the concussion of struggle and construct
little images from day to day, little votive figures around the
crater of the world that help conceal and perhaps control its
violence.

But it was the days they were not together, when he had to
work overtime or was committed elsewhere, which were the
empty pockets in the magic ball, the disconcerting realization
that another life was winding itself into view like a dim,
emergent spool in the sky. For now he had begun to Be in Rio,
having become slowly involved in a system of social attraction

208

with contending centers and evolving whorls. "Damn it all, Léa. I can't see you tonight," he found himself saying every now and then. "I've got to go to the Carneiro's. He's a Minister you know, and the Admiral thinks it's good relations for us to get around."

Sometimes he made excuses when it was not absolutely necessary for he was beginning to find the accelerating suction of their life together too all-absorbing. He loved Léa, he did not want to hurt her, but it grew in his mind like a strand of thought attached to that other evolving world that it might not turn out as they had hoped. It was for this reason that he held back, that he would not have an affair with her though the moment of easy possession was long since past—he would not, in any case, be of the "love 'em and leave 'em" variety. Sometimes, and perhaps this was the trouble, his idealization of her dimmed, and though she was still the finest which her world produced, he felt he was looking at her through a perspective of history and that he could have loved her completely only by standing still for two hundred years and waiting for her. She wanted him to advance, of course, as she herself was moving, but she didn't see that they lived in different worlds of time. If he had not wanted to go on ahead, she would have loved him as he was, for to her he had already nearly reached the end of dreaming, and it was this willing tranquillity of her love and friendship which troubled him in the bitterest paradox of all that one's friend could be the enemy.

It was inevitable that Buck's other life and the life he shared with Léa should through maladroit circumstances touch in passing, for Léa was neither altogether in nor out of society. As the daughter of an Admiral, it was protocol that she should be invited to the large cocktail party given by the Naval Attaché at his plush apartment in the Copacabana, and Buck, who had not seen her in several days, felt with a kind of premonitive uneasiness that she would be there and would take a long, sweet,

209

patient look at what it was that had now begun to make him seem like a man with twin souls trying to move in opposite directions.

When he arrived, he saw that it was to be the type of party he had been going to a good deal lately with his *gran fino* friends. It had the setting: a large, oval drawing room, softly lit, flower-bedecked—a glowing, murmuring containment against the discordancies and crudities of the world outside. Yes, of late, he had learned to warm himself in these lambent centers which every evening glimmered like jewels in the twilight of the city.

Looking around, he saw Léa coming toward him, plainly dressed, a little awkwardly so, it now seemed to him. "Hello, Buck. So there you are," she said. "I'm so glad to see you. We've been missing you at home, Papa, Mama, Laura, and I. When you don't come by, we've nothing to do—you can't imagine. We just sit around and talk *Americanismo*."

"Well, I sure am sorry, Léa. I meant to call you, but I was called out of town unexpectedly on business for the Navy. I was going to phone you tonight. We've got some catching up to do." He winked and smiled at her, stringing several little lies together. Why not? He loved . . . liked the girl, and wanted to spare her any hurt feelings.

Maluh Bueno Prado, one of his new friends, came up to them. She had been at Vassar but there was nothing collegiate about her, and she must have seemed rather like a visiting Countess among the other students with her dark hair, white skin, aquamarine eyes, and expensive clothes.

"There you are at last, Buck darling," she said, and it was apparent that she would move on in a moment like one of the unacknowledged hostesses of the party. "I've been looking everywhere for you. I wanted to tell you not to forget about tonight. About eight-thirty at my house, remember?" She suddenly recognized his companion. "Oh, hello, Léa. Charming to see you. I didn't know you were home. We must have tea together some afternoon and gossip about the States. Do give me a call, dear."

210

As he stood between them, balancing his cocktail somewhat awkwardly, he wondered if the color of his confusion had spread over his face, feeling the rays of their personalities cross him while he looked through and beyond. But Maluh smoothly blended the situation for them all. "Come along," she said. "You just can't monopolize each other. I must share you with my friends." And then they were circulating which gave him no trouble for he knew it as more or less an American invention.

He looked around at his compatriots, the Navy men in their white dress uniforms towering over the shorter Brazilians, and their wives, also taller, lacking the suppliant femininity of the Brazilian women, and he could see that they were doing a good job of getting around, sometimes almost too much so, as though they of all people hated most to get stuck. Looking from one side of the room to the other, they paused restively to acknowledge their companions from time to time, but kept on the lookout for whoever might be embedded in the crowd. Buck, to whom this had always been hateful, suddenly saw it as not necessarily so odious—it was a nervous habit performed by many who secretly thought the whole affair rather silly, who wanted to get on with the thing. It was a symbol of national loneliness—Americans wanted to meet everybody, to see everything. The best of them belonged to themselves alone somewhere at home, behind their official manners—you could see it in their faces. But cocktail parties were where you had to go to see the people who would help you get things done. Yet they did not fall for all of this like the *gran finos,* and they were not afraid of it like Léa. For the first time in years, he saw himself among them—many were like himself—they also "walked between."

After the little revelatory thrill of union, he squired the two girls around easily, moving with them in the revolving tub of color, scent, and music. It did not make him dizzy any more. At any moment he could bring it to a stasis, step outside the heart of the jewel, knowing he could crush it to its components like an imitation, letting the colored dust sift through his fingers, sieving, here and there, an enduring crystal. The admiralty of

the world loved such brilliance—let them have it, let them foun-
der in its delusive light, and let those who loved its grace and
desirability with candor, as he still did, see it as something the
world wore as a gem of its Becoming.

It would have been hard for Buck to say later exactly when
Léa relinquished him. Without her help, it would have had to
be a break on his part, and he could never have quite forgiven
himself for that. One day, she accepted the fact of a growing
distance, simply, with the tenderness of doom which she dis-
guised in ironical gaiety. "Well, Buck, you're becoming *ele-
gante,* very *gran fino.* I read about you in the papers all the
time," she said, releasing him to the parties and the people
which had become a counter-pole of his life. Whenever he
wanted to see her, she was always willing, but they would usually
sit together for a long time without saying anything as though
a language, perhaps the right one, were longing to be born, as
though, if only they held the globe there between them and
turned it with their hands fast enough, all the continents would
merge in the congruency of a rainbow glow.

But, though Léa helped him all she could, Buck knew that
there was no such thing as good-bye to a girl like her whose
sense of waiting and perseverance denied at the very moment
that it granted him farewell. How could anyone ever say good-
bye to the good no matter how it seemed to enchain him with
gentle hands? It was life that finally stepped in, as he remembered it had done so often before, until he had developed in a
rudimentary way what he would have called with a nostalgic
smile "a sense of destiny." When he received his notice that he
was to be shipped back to the States for further assignment, he
was thankful for the progression of a world behind his individual devotions and personal dreams.

There was not much to say to Léa—he could offer her nothing,
he could promise her nothing. He felt overwhelmingly that he
had been the receiver though she would have told him no. She
had slowed him down, steadied him, given him depth. He had

212

come to Brazil with a grudge against the world, a quarrel in his throat, and she was sending him back a lover. In a strange way she had made him a better American. He had turned away from his country with a scowl, and now he was returning as though it received him with the enigmatic smile of all its daring dreams. Wasn't it Léa, after all, who had made him see America as one of the loveliest works in progress? Hadn't she taught him too that your enemy may also be your friend?

Their leave-taking was to be short and sweet—she as well as he would want it that way. On the eve of his departure, he stopped by and found her much as she was on the first evening at her home, unaffectedly glad to see him, trapped in a little air of native sorrow. The family were ceremonious, tactful, like dark parentheses around her luminous sadness, soon withdrawing to the interior of the house.

He had brought her a topaz ring as a going-away present. When she put it on her finger, it shone in the light like a prism of tawny-gold.

"Oh, Buck," she said. "It's beautiful. But you shouldn't have done it. It is I who should be giving you something. It is I who will be grateful always."

"But Léa—"he began. "Can you, will you believe that—" But he would not finish so easily with "I shall be back?". That would have been the worst of lies spoken as they rose on a crest of feeling.

She took his hand, lightly brushing his lips with hers, and quickly, firmly, finished the *despedida*. *"Boa viagem,* Buck, And *boa sorte,* good luck always."

Back at the apartment when he had finished packing his bags, feeling drunk and bludgeoned with his departure, he went out on the balcony to take a last look at the lights of Rio—*a cidade maravilhosa,* the marvelous city. Ridiculous! It was not just Rio —it was all of Brazil—it was the marvelous land! So diverse, so fertile in contrast that it baffled the mind and sometimes es- tranged the heart. It was the country of God's exhaustion where divine defeat brooded in the unformed *mélange* of man and

213

nature: the incredible beauty of the landscape in places, its barrenness or strangling lushness in others . . . the cities . . . Rio, lavish, seductive, misleading, São Paulo of rugged and unpolished strength . . . and the others, the primitive, mouldering, sometimes menacing cities like half-shaped artifacts left for some greater effort of the hand. Spirit moved freer with present skill in other lands, but perhaps it had left here its most passionate shapes, its most thunderous colors, as a gigantic promise of a world to be.

He heard a strain of samba float up to him and he looked down and saw a street group dancing. They were the ones who had inherited God's massive scene, and down there at the bottom of it all like prisoners of its beauty, bounty, and their bewildering opposites, they were making music, rooting themselves in the best way they knew. They smiled and beckoned to him with hands the color of earth. He could have thrown them his heart if, if, if . . .

He thought of Léa and how she would have called down to them and tossed them a flower out of natural affinity. As he went in and lay on his bed, he could think of nothing but her, and it seemed that her image made a niche in the air for itself, brown and glowing, a darkness hovering with light, surely as he remembered her first with the eternal, golden-grieving smile of a Madonna which was a gateway, a door, that had once turned inward but now seemed outward-giving as though it wished for the wisher what he loved.